NAMEDROPPER

A NOVEL

EMMA FORREST

SCRIBNER PAPERBACK FICTION
Published by Simon & Schuster
NEW YORK LONDON TORONTO SYDNEY SINGAPORE

SCRIBNER PAPERBACK FICTION
Simon & Schuster, Inc.
Rockefeller Center
1230 Avenue of the Americas
New York, NY 10020

First published in the UK in 1998 by Arrow Books Limited

SCRIBNER PAPERBACK FICTION and design are trademarks of
Macmillan Library Reference USA, Inc., used under license
by Simon & Schuster, the publisher of this work.

Designed by Colin Joh
Set in Electra

Manufactured in the United States of America

1 3 5 7 9 10 8 6 4 2

Library of Congress Cataloging-in-Publication Data
Forrest, Emma.
Namedropper : a novel / Emma Forrest.
— 1st Scribner Paperback Fiction ed.
p. cm.
1. Teenage girls—England—Fiction. I. Title.
PR6056.O6836 N36 2000
823'.914—dc21   99-088008

.   ISBN 0-684-86538-6

For E. Paul Sevigny, who tried to wash me clean

Special thanks to Mum and Dad, Kim Witherspoon, my editor Carrie Thornton, Josh Greenhut, Felicity Rubinstein, Ashley Feinstein, Louise Lasser, Len and Alice, Bobbi and Larry, Minnie and Josh, the Rosenblums, Annabel, Bay, Rachel Weisz, Chloë and Janine, Toby Amies, Amanda Claff, Jason Isaly, Michel Galen, Alan Fraser, and the 394 Pony Pep Squad.

"As Elizabeth was leaving she gave her mother a quick kiss and said 'Oh, Mother! Nick and I are now one for ever and ever'"

—Elizabeth Taylor, The Last Star, Kitty Kelley

ONE

He was a super-shiny boy and I liked the shape of him. Under the blanket. In the shower. I liked his shadow on the street and his imprint on the sofa. I hated the smell of hair gel on his head, but I loved it on the pillow. I love the smell of losing someone. From the time I met him, he left me little clues of a man, a trail of bread crumbs to a gingerbread cottage. Inside the cottage were peeling pictures of Elizabeth Taylor and Marilyn Monroe that keep sliding to the floor because the walls were too sweet to hold the Blu-Tack. I tried to pick the posters off the floor and got so distracted, I ended up in an oven. So I climbed out of the oven and out of the house and I was saving myself, but it hurt so bad. I found the boy I loved, but he didn't want to hug me because I was blistered and spotted with bread crumbs. I looked up close because, up close, I could always see myself reflected in the surface of his shiny, iconic beauty. But suddenly he had pores, grey hairs, and chapped lips. And I couldn't see a damn thing.

Treena doesn't want to know about boys or pain or pictures of dead actresses. The irony being that Treena has the looks of a silver-screen goddess. She doesn't know the films of Marilyn Monroe, but she thinks she knows who I'm talking about. She can picture a blonde from the olden days. "Dead blonde?"

she asks, making it sound like a new shade of hair dye. She hasn't seen any Elizabeth Taylor movies either, but, from my walls, she knows that she's the one with black hair, who's still alive. Treena definitely hasn't heard of Ava Gardner, Cyd Charisse, Gina Lollobrigida, Jane Russell, or Lauren Bacall, but I have and that's all that matters.

Treena is her own movie goddess. Even when she's asleep, she is the Eve Arnold photo of Marilyn Monroe dressed in leopard print, lying on her tummy in the bull rushes. She never works out or reads a book, but her body and mind stay firm—African bottom, Swedish porno breasts, and blond curly hair emerging from curly thoughts. If I tell her she should read this novel, or that autobiography, she holds it in her hand for a minute, weighing it up and down, and then passes it back, smirking. "There, read it. You're right. It was good."

First-year girls don't want to look like Treena. They think she looks rude. The girls at school who are considered pretty look like colts in cults, all gangly limbs and blank expressions. They read *Cosmopolitan* and don't eat. Treena has to eat a pound of salad a day or she can't sleep. She eats it *because she likes the taste*.

She's always lived next door to the hardest state school in North London. Every now and then the school kids try to beat her up for being too pretty. Walking up Parkway, past the toy shop with the angry dog outside, along the grungy pubs populated by spitty old men and teenage girls wearing peep-toe stilettos in the dead of winter, it's just too scary to face Treena. You feel you ought to hit her, or hide her. I've wanted to. She doesn't *have* to walk like that, so arrogant and sexy. She doesn't have to glare "I know" under the lashes of her long green eyes. She needn't laugh at the common people as they scuttle by.

"What do you think of him?" I'll ask, pointing at a bowl-haired bassist from some indie band or other. "No thank you! He's got a *Star Trek* haircut. He looks like a Romulan." Suddenly, her attention is focused on him and she calls across the street, "Hey, monkey Romulan, sort it out!"

As we turn on to Camden Lock and the market, my nose wrinkles up, assaulted by the foul odour of incense and half-cooked hot dogs. Treena loves it, never tires of the racks of tie-dyed dungarees and rows of flowery Doc Martens. Every day she makes us late for school, thumbing through the boxes of seven inches and knock-off cassettes.

"Veeve, have you got any money?"

"Not for a Steely Dan record, I don't."

Now, there is no reason for a seventeen-year-old girl to like the stuff she likes. It's not like she's influenced by her parents' records, because all they have is dinner-party music—George Michael and Seal. Treena likes her hip-hop, knows it inside out, shakes her head, sighing, "I can't believe you've never heard Run DMC's first album." She gets it from her suitors, who are almost always DJs and club promoters. But every now and then she has these inexplicable blips. It's like she came out of a pod liking Steely Dan.

Even when she buys really tacky shit, it never drags her down. She forks out three pounds for a crappy cannabis-leaf earring, but she carries it off like it's Tiffany's. She is an irredeemable peace-and-love chick, which proves how dumb she is. She's not interested in the politics and mechanics of love and peace, just the enamel-plated peace-sign ankle chain. That is her gesture for world peace, and she means it with the utmost sincerity.

She'll sign any petition presented to us between her house and school: Anti-Nazi League, Anti-Vivisection League, Anti-Israel, Anti-Palestine. She'll give her change to the Lifeboat Institute or the Scientologists, whoever asks her for a donation first. A charity tin is a charity tin. She believes what people tell her.

When her brother was born, her parents tried their best to make their hyper little girl feel a part of the event. "Tom is our gift to you."

"Thank you," said Treena, plucking him from his crib in the half minute her mother was out of the room, and depositing him neatly in the push bin. "I don't like him. He doesn't work. I want a real one, a Cabbage Patch Kid."

Treena doesn't have that many friends apart from me and Marcus, who she met at a Wu-Tang Clan gig at The Rocket and who has been in love with her ever since. He doesn't say a lot, maybe "a'ight?" or a nervous-sounding "Peace," as if he is genuinely expecting war to break out. It seems like he wants to say more, but this is all his position will allow him, the same way Michael Jackson may want to address his fans truthfully, but all he ever does is wave and squeak "I love you!"

I've never had a real conversation with Marcus. When we pass in Treena's hallway, he nods and sometimes smiles, flashing teeth so bright white and ostentatious gold, they look like a Versace outfit. Marcus has a long, slim nose with a bump at the top like a tortoise-shell cat. His lids are heavy and his bottom lip is thicker than his top lip. He's a very good-looking

boy. He could have any fly girl he wanted. But he wants
Treena. He is kind to her, rings her every day after school,
rings her before she goes to sleep, sends her funny postcards
for no reason, takes her to dinner whenever he can afford it
and whenever he can't afford it. He worships and adores her.
And she hates him for it. She hates it so much that she refuses
to acknowledge his feelings, not even to me. Amongst the
hate crimes she has committed against him:

1. Urinated on the carpeted floor of his bedroom because
   she was too lazy to go to the bathroom.
2. Spat cranberry juice in his eyes because DJ Flex had
   given her cystitis and she wanted Marcus to be as sore as
   she was.
3. Had him stroke her hand when she was vomiting all
   night from the morning-after pill necessitated by her
   one-night stand with the aforementioned DJ.

As she jabbers away, he just watches her. Raised on the first
London estate to fall to crack, he is less frightened of Treena
than most people who meet her.

A beautiful woman is scary enough. But a beautiful, crazy
person . . . it's too much. They are bad luck. They are Marilyn, Frances Farmer, and Blanche DuBois. They are not nice
to be around. Treena's saving grace is that her eccentricities
are thoroughly unfeminine. It's a very masculine craziness.
No nervous neuroses, no facial ticks and Valium. Just all-out,
blow-the-whole-joint-up lunacy. When she was thirteen, she
tried to make some extra money baby-sitting for the couple
across the street, but it didn't work out.

"I'm sorry, I don't think I can baby-sit again. I wanted to kill your children," she explained, smoothing her blouse.

"Oh, dear," gasped the mortified mother. "Were they really that naughty?"

"Oh, no," smiled Treena, "not at all. They went to bed at eight and slept like lambs. But about nine, I got the urge to kill them, and I had to grip the sides of the sofa to stop myself from going into the kitchen and picking up a knife. It's passed now. Nevertheless, it's probably best not to ask me round while you're out."

She tried work as a hairdresser's assistant, but was appalled when the customers had fixed ideas of how they wanted to look.

"Really, you'll look better with short red hair, I promise. You have quite an ugly face. It will distract attention from it." Before she could be fired, she stormed out, disgusted that she was expected to sweep the clumps of hacked hair from the floor.

She has no sense of there being different leagues. She'd pick a fight with Mike Tyson if she thought he was looking at her funny. She doesn't think that because she is on a scholarship she has any duty to perform well academically, or even behave well. Exam after exam, she lays her head on the paper and naps, or spends the hour and a half doodling. Nothing offensive, just a cheery, balloon-lettered "HELLO!" to the examiner, or a cartoon of a pig with long eyelashes.

Treena's real name is Katerina. She is Swedish but takes it with good grace. I don't mind her being a blonde because at least she sticks by it, she knows what she is. One ought to be proud of one's hair colour and be the best blonde/brunette/

redhead one can be. That's the trouble with America today—
their sex symbols have no hair colour. What colour is Jennifer
Aniston's hair? That really pisses me off.

Treena tosses her golden ringlets over her five-foot-nine
frame, raises a defined eyebrow over a kitty-kat eye, smacks
her Clara Bow lips beneath an aristocratic nose, and sighs as if
being gorgeous was not a task to be undertaken lightly. The
teachers try very hard not to look at her. She doesn't see her
height or weight or breasts as being in any way restricting her
adventures. She doesn't understand that she's a girl and she's
supposed to be afraid of striking up conversations with
drunken gangs of football fans holding broken bottles or of
cutting through parks alone at night. She's so confident about
her right to be there that the boys address her politely and
even the ill-lit parks back down.

It's all in her walk, a cartoon swagger, part Jayne Mans-
field, part Muhammad Ali. Men never know if it is an invitation upstairs or an invitation outside. You should see her
strutting through the underpass from Marcus's council house
to the tube. The cracked walls of the tunnel quake as she
approaches and the bricks seem to stare as she passes.

Two

Once, I convinced myself I was in love with Ray, my other best pal. He's a pop star. It lasted almost two weeks, smack in the middle of August. At first I thought it was the strident London heat that was making my head pound. The fact that I always felt too hot when I was with Ray in his house, I put down to the radiators that still hummed in his room, long after winter had handed in its notice, sick of being overworked and unloved. Ray couldn't stand to let it go and left the heat on low, as if to entice February back. He knew it wouldn't happen, but it was a tradition for him, like leaving a place for Elijah.

I loved that about Ray—that the summer terrified him, made him feel he had even less space on this earth than usual. What with all the flowers and bumblebees and picnic goers, he feared he would become invisible, lost in the Versace patterns of the season. In winter, with the trees stripped to their Helmut Lang basics, he felt he had less to compete with. The chill suited him. He knew he looked best with a nice biting north wind holding his wavy dark hair behind him, like bridesmaids carrying a train. It also allowed him to dress up as Russian aristocracy, in a long, swinging coat and black leather gloves.

Ray is adopted. He was raised by a kind, dull couple in the countryside and he has not kept in contact with them or the countryside. He hates parks, trees, and plants in bloom, and summer because it encourages them all. It makes no sense to turn up the radiator to combat the summer, but it was his warped idea of defiance and he stomped around the flat cursing all eighty-one degrees and watching Woody Allen videos.

Ray thinks he may be Italian or Greek. From the mass of hair that springs from his head, I think he may be right. Thirty-three years old and he still has the thickest, darkest hair of any man I've met. Hair loss is the most fundamental worry of men throughout the Western world, and I get the impression Ray almost resents not having that additional fear. For Ray, anxiety is freedom. He's always whining, "Am I fat? Am I fat?" And most of the time, he's just stocky. But in some photos he does look like he's just slaughtered a pig and eaten it whole. When I first met Ray, he was running five miles a day and his body was ripped. He's stopped running lately and has gone a little to seed.

Like I say, I wouldn't have noticed that I was thinking of Ray romantically, except one Saturday, when he ripped off his T-shirt in the kitchen, exasperated at the lazy, gluey heat sticking to his armpits. As he balled up the damp cotton in his fist, I caught myself sneaking a look at his chest. Before, I would just *look* at him changing. It was the sneakiness that got me. He began to look different and I began to put on eye shadow before I saw him.

I had just got back my essay on D. H. Lawrence. I loved his books, but the only way I could express how much I loved them was by comparing *Lady Chatterley's Lover* to the video for "Uptown Girl" by Billy Joel. Car mechanic falls in love with uptown girl, does synchronised dance routine to impress her. Billy Joel/Mellors, Lady Chatterley/Christie Brinkley— same thing. Basically, I'm a snob and a terrible person, but, like Manny, I have always liked working-class men.

I think a man ought, if he can help it, to be working class. And men should also be of Celtic descent where at all possible. And ladies should be Mediterranean. My dreams are populated by men who look like Gabriel Byrne and talk like Dick Van Dyke and women who look like Sophia Loren but are dubbed by Helena Bonham-Carter. I don't care if it's their genuine accent or not. I don't see what's so good about being genuine. Clog dancing is genuine. Isn't being fake more of an achievement? At least it takes some inspiration. Like, sherbet dips, they're a special food. Think of all the additives and colouring and grinding that it takes to create a sherbet dip. But carrots? They're just out there, shrieking, "Hi, we're some carrots! Love us for it!" They never have to prove themselves. They are the Gwyneth Paltrow of the food world. They'd make the most stylish vegetable list, even wearing a pink ball-gown three sizes too big.

When I got into D. H. Lawrence, I went to the library and checked out three books at once, winking at the librarian and whispering, "Sex," as I took them from her. It was whilst going back over *The Virgin and the Gypsy* that I started to notice just how common Ray was. Every hair between his brows seemed defined. His sweat began to smell of hard manual labour as opposed to poncing around in Islington wine bars.

Ray and I met at the Tate Gallery, in front of the portrait of Ophelia drowning, which just about says it all. He sidled up next to me. One always thinks one ought to be attracted to any young person by themselves in an art gallery, especially if they're wearing a black turtleneck. When he got up close, I don't think he liked the look of me so much. But he chatted politely anyway. I pretended I didn't know who he was. He pretended he liked that, but I could tell he really didn't.

His pretentious sensory perceptors alerted him to a kindred soul. I was so happy to meet someone more pretentious than me—pretentious and succesful. I would be far kinder to him if he hadn't sold so many records and made so much money. The more he sells, the more I taunt him. I like taunting him. It's so easy. One time he told me that people think he looks like Edward Norton. I said, "Edward Norton is much better-looking than you." Ray turned absolutely indignant with rage and bellowed, "NO HE IS NOT!" Which is just not a thing a person is supposed to say out loud, and that's why I love him. Sometimes I think Ray just keeps me around to help him keep track of who he hates.

"Veeve, babe. Who's that guy from *Good Will Hunting* that I hate?"

"Matt Damon?"

"No, the other one."

"Ben Affleck?"

"Yeah, Ben Affleck. I hate him."

What Ray and I have is affection through word association. "Truffaut?" "Me too" "Love you." Reality is matted and ugly and I didn't want to bring any real love into this gorgeous all-surface, no-feeling relationship we have going.

So one evening, the night before he was due to perform at an awards ceremony in Europe, I decided to put a stop to it. I had been thinking about him all through my girls' night in with Treena, all through Treena's lunchtime babble, all through dinner with Manny at the new Chinese restaurant on Greek Street. So I called him a little after midnight.

"Ray, Ray, it's me. Listen, I just want to say that even though you're very handsome, I don't find you at all attractive."

I think I heard him start to clear his throat, so I quickly added: "That red raincoat that you think makes you look really cool makes you look like the killer dwarf from *Don't Look Now.* When you stand on the outskirts of a crowded party, watching everyone with your arms folded against your chest, thinking you look like an existential hero, everyone else thinks you look like a grumpy troll. Good luck for tomorrow. Bye."

I immediately felt much better. Ray did not come across as his usual brooding love-god self the next day on TV. When he picked up his award for best album, he didn't thank Woody Allen for inspiration or send a Red Indian girl to turn it down. He just said thank you very politely and scuttled offstage. He was wearing a purple, crushed velvet, tightly tailored suit, and you could see in his eyes that the moment he walked onstage, he realised the suit was a mistake. That wasn't like him.

Ray, like all the most attractive people, is a chancer. You sit there taking him apart, saying, "Well, this doesn't work and this doesn't work, so why is he such a sex symbol?" and it's because he's decided to be. And, when a chancer backs down, you have to face the fact that you've been lied to and that you enjoy being lied to, that it took the pressure off the quest to really love, to really feel. When a chancer admits he has taken one chance too many, you realise you could have had the same feelings for a lip-gloss, if you had put your mind to it. And you would want to be with the lip-gloss as much as possible, and sit by the phone waiting for it to call, refuse to share the lip-gloss with others, and fall absolutely to pieces when the pot of gloss is empty.

Pots of gloss wouldn't sing as badly as Ray, like a Laandan Cockernee, even though he's from Surrey. I hate Ray's music. It's soulless soul. He's more interested in telling the world about the contents of his record collection than in actually making a good record. He always gets nervous a month before release and throws on a load of strings. This costs the record company thousands, but he makes them a lot of money. Everyone likes him, from *Q* readers to *Smash Hits* readers. The *Smash Hits* readers are more vocal, so much so that they're threatening to alienate the *Q* readers.

I don't like any of his records, and even if I started to, I wouldn't let myself until at least five years after our friendship ends. I only start to like a song about five years after it's been a big hit.

Anyone who does not think that "Boys of Summer" by Don Henley is a brilliant record is someone I'd definitely hate. Manny always taught me that the only people I was allowed to hate were Adolf Hitler, Margaret Thatcher, and Jack Lemmon. Hitler because he destroyed our people. Thatcher because she destroyed our country. I don't know why he took against Jack Lemmon so. He'd only say, "Jack Lemmon makes me anxious."

"Boys of Summer" is a song that stops me dead whenever it

comes on the radio. It's happened in the back of cabs, in the supermarket, doing the washing up. It makes me want to kill myself, but I never turn it off, and if I can't hear it all the way through, I think I will die, and by the time the last notes fade out, I want to live forever.

"I can't tell you my love for you will still be strong, after the boys of summer have gone."

I think that's such a beautiful sentiment. Love should only last as long as a very expensive and impractical bikini that looks stunning but dissolves in the sea within days. So many pop songs tell of this terrible tiresome love that they want to last forever. But that just makes me think of long-life milk, acrid and fake. Love should be like a movie trailer. Even if the film's a stinker, you get the best laughs and the biggest explosions in the space of two minutes.

Manny doesn't like it. We have been through it and it turns out that he is bothered by the lyric "Out on the road today I saw a Deadhead sticker on a Cadillac." Manny says that implies that there's something inherently wrong about being an arty liberal and wealthy at the same time. That's what we are.

We're arty liberals, champagne socialists. My first year was spent in New York. Then, when my grandparents were run over by a limo after watching a Debbie Reynolds musical revue in Las Vegas, Manny inherited a lot of money. Mom collected her half, dumped me, and went on the first of many Buddhist retreats, taking her worldly possessions but abandoning all family connections. Manny took his half and me, and moved us from New York to London to be closer to Ava

Gardner, who ended up dying in West London before they could consummate his decades-long imaginary friendship.

Manny bought our house for a remarkable price and did it up himself. The four storeys are done out in black and gold, apart from the guest bedroom, which is black and red (the Polanski suite). There are Tiffany lamps on every table and I've tripped over the wires so many times that the shades are beyond repair. There are no bannisters in our house, so we don't do a lot of running. Apart from Treena, who always falls off from halfway down, but never fails to land on her feet.

There are framed photos going up the stairs of Elizabeth Taylor in various stages of husbandry and fatitude. Manny touches the portraits on his way to the bathroom. He always does it, as if they were mezuzahs. Consequently the *Place in the Sun*–era Liz sits at a jaunty angle and Liz in her white swimsuit filming *Suddenly, Last Summer* is covered in fingerprints. We always have Elizabeth to turn to. Even in black-and-white, her eyes glow violet. There are moments in your life that no metaphysical poem or prayer or Leonard Cohen lyric can cut through. But Liz's eyes do. They can cut through anything. And, on evenings like these, when our hearts feel tight and the rain beats rudely, an incessant, vulgar splash against the serenity of our sadness, Liz's bosom heaves with us.

In the dead of night, a couple of days before New Year's Eve 1988, I thought I heard Manny pray to her. That was the year he had split up with Miguel. No one ever dumped Liz. Sure, she had a lot of marriages, but she never got dumped. He seemed to pep up not long after their little chat. At Christmas, he leaves a saucer of vanilla-bean ice cream with Hershey's syrup in front of each picture. Manny says we're all going to lose our figures anyway, and if it's good enough for Liz . . .

She is the Mommy of this house and I have grown up in her image. Not nearly as beautiful, but like a bad Internet printout of her. I have almost-black hair and navy-blue eyes that I try to wish purple. Elizabeth wished herself two inches taller in order to get the lead in *National Velvet*. My skin is so pale that people would think Manny was feeding me feathers if I weren't so fat. Manny says I am not fat. He says I am voluptuous. I don't feel voluptuous. I feel like a cow and I have recurring dreams about running to do a big leap and then not being able to lift myself off the ground because I'm too heavy. On a good day, I know I'm not *fat* fat. I'm somewhere between Madonna in the "Lucky Star" video and Drew Barrymore pre-comeback. Or Elizabeth Taylor in *Butterfield 8*. I have these boobs and this butt that are just separate from me, like they're having a conversation with each other and I'm not allowed to join in. My own body makes me feel like I'm alone.

It doesn't make sense because my mother was totally flat-chested. That's probably why all Manny's photos of her show her wearing some stupid spaghetti-strap hippie dress without a bra. She's super-thin with long red hair trailing down her bony back. I hate hair that goes on that long—it's just belabouring the point.

I don't miss her. I never knew her, so there isn't a problem. There are all those men who are totally fucked up about women because their mum walked out when they were six, but I don't feel any of that. It's like being blind—if you're born that way, you don't know any different and you don't miss out, but if you lose your sight at the age of thirty-eight, your life is shattered. Besides, Manny, who has taught me to always judge a book by its cover, is the greatest role model a girl could hope for.

Last time my mother came out of the Buddhist retreat, she tried to set up a reunion with me. But I didn't want to meet her. She'd been in a Buddhist retreat for five years. I know she wouldn't have heard of Ben Affleck and that it would just annoy me.

If I'm absolutely honest with myself, which I am when it's three in the morning and I still can't sleep, I do look for mother figures everywhere. Not because I want one. Because I'm curious. Because I can't get my head around it. I'm a tiny bit obsessed by the idea of mothers, the same way I'm obsessed by the idea of a jar that contains both peanut butter and jelly in one spread.

When I'm paying the checkout lady, I think, "Oh, she's a mother," like "Oh, she's a Mormon." It's just something some women are. I see it as a cult. It shouldn't be outlawed, but you don't really want to let them into your house. Most girls are daughters. It's something they have to be, whether they like it or not, another burden when it's already enough work just being a girl, then a teenage girl, let alone a teenage girl who belongs to someone else. Luckily I don't have that. I think I'd feel like a split personality if I had a mom. I would call her Mom and not Mother, which makes me think of Jane Austen, or Mommy, which makes me think of Joan Crawford.

Mom said Manny could care for me better than she ever could and she was right. I think she found herself. Every now and then we get a postcard from an artists' colony in Topanga

Canyon, an Israeli kibbutz, or a monastery in the south of France. If I found myself, I'd say, "Well, there you are, Viva, so nice to meet you," and then I'd go back to bed. I don't think about her. I think about pasta in the shape of Hello Kitty, stockings with diamond seams up the back, Marilyn's crumbling cake-mascara, and Liz Taylor's new white hair. I haven't got time for the trivials.

THREE

I was always a highly strung child. I had to take eleven days off school when I was five after Uncle Manny took me to see *Bambi*. Four years later I was still undergoing therapy for separation trauma brought on by the scene where Bambi's mother is shot by a hunter. This was not an uncommon phobia at the time. In nursery, I became friendly with a boy called "Superman Jeff" who wore his pants over his trousers and cried when his mother dropped him off because it reminded him of baby Superman being sent to earth as his planet exploded around him. Still, he was not nearly as traumatised as me. At least Superman's mum and dad came to life as holograms of Marlon Brando and Susannah York. Bambi's was dead, full stop, no deer hologram. No magic powers. Shot by hunters with nary a Gucci deer jacket to show for it.

I liked the idea of therapy—it was something I had heard Woody Allen talk highly of. I could tell Manny was worried that everyone would think I was a five-year-old freak because he kept saying, "If you have a session that clashes with a lesson, just tell your friends you have to go to Hebrew class."

"No way," I choked, "that's so embarrassing," and every time I had an appointment I'd raise my hand and say, as loudly as I could, "Miss Matthews, I have to be excused. I have an appointment with my therapist."

She'd blush and whisper, "Oh, your *therapist*," as if "therapist" were actually a code word for "Hebrew lesson."

Uncle Manny looked after me in the eleven days I was away from school, in self-enforced Bambi exile. He drew me a cartoon strip of *Crime and Punishment* to read, so my education wouldn't suffer. I wriggled about on Manny's boyfriend's lap whilst he was trying to read an E. M. Forster biography, and lay my head on the page so my chocolate curls obscured the writing.

Now here I am, seventeen with a bullet, failing school miserably, even the subjects I'm good at. The bullshit classes. The ones I can talk my way out of. English, Art, Classics, History, Religious Studies. Sample Religious Studies question: "Is racism a good thing or a bad thing?" It's enough to make you become a Klansman, just so the answer will be less dull to write; and the two black girls in my class feel the same. I just can't be bothered to answer anymore. I expect to fail Maths, Biology, French. I fully intend to. But even I am a little ashamed about being bottom of the class in Religious Studies.

We're sitting our mocks at the moment. School is mocking me. Not just the kids and the teachers, but the timbers that hold the building upright. The end-of-year exams are a big deal. They determine whether or not you go to university. I don't want to go to university. I don't like unity and I hate verses—I just love the chorus of songs. I have no motivation because they can't threaten me with not getting into college since I don't want to go anyway. College is for people who want to extend their childhood for as long as possible. Education really doesn't come into it. The only way I get through school is to pretend it's a set-up for a musical number. As I talk to Treena, or listen to Madame, I am working out where the song is going to come in.

You know: "I am so enjoying getting to know you . . . *Getting to know you!*" or "My goodness, we've talked so long it's now the next morning. And what a lovely morning . . . *Good morning!*" On the walk home from school, I wonder what's going to inspire that policeman over there to start dancing, or when Frank Sinatra's going to come careering round the bend dressed as a sailor. It's never when I expect. Then, back at the house, I put on full makeup and drink coffee because that's when I know the cameras are really on me.

"Gosh," sniffs Manny, "you look like Ava Gardner today."

I scrunch a wedge of dark-brown hair from my cheek and bite my lip. Sometimes I worry I might be really homophobic and then I remember, no, I just hate Manny. "You always say that."

"No I don't. Usually I say you look like Elizabeth Taylor, but today you look like Ava Gardner. There is a Southern fire in your eyes. You look like you've just made love to a bull-fighter!"

"How can you say that when you know I just sat through a two-hour math class?" I howl.

I don't like the whole "Oh, you know who you look like?" thing. First off, it's usually not true. When Manny says I look like Ava Gardner, what he really means is, I have dark hair. When he says my mother looked like Rita Hayworth, what he's trying to tell me is that she had red hair. Or that we have

31

Alzheimer's in the family and that's the kindest way he can think of to say it. I wouldn't be surprised. My first memory is of my mother giving me cat food and giving the cat my mushed meatloaf.

If it is true, if you really do look like someone, well, that's even worse. How terribly sad it must be to actually look a bit like Daniel Day-Lewis, but not as handsome, or something like Isabelle Adjani, but not quite. How could you live with yourself?

Because Manny is gay, we never had that icky part where I developed breasts and he freaked out and didn't want to hug me anymore. Instead, he points them out at every occasion: "Stand back, Viva, you're going to poke my eyes out." "Even when you were eight years old," he gushes, "even when you were flat as a board, you were just such a woman!" When I did get a figure, he just went crazy for it, like if I never did another thing in my life, I've made him as proud as he could possibly be. He buys me fancy fifties gear—vintage pointy stuff—and takes a lot of care hand-washing them. Not even Treena is wearing a suspender belt under her regulation A-line skirt.

I'm trying to read over my History notes. The garter belt is making me nervous. I clamp my legs tight together and tug at the grey flannel skirt that scratches my legs. The unnatural fibres of the skirt lap at the tops of my exposed thighs like a one-night stand you don't want to touch you in the morning. The train clunks gingerly up the line, a supermodel descending the runway in six-inch platform shoes. I place my satchel on my knees and flex my thigh muscles so that any hint of underwear is obscured. I'm always convinced that the person in the seat opposite is trying to look up my skirt. It's usually a seventy-year-old Granny happily ensconced in a book called *World of Crocheting,* but it doesn't stop me worrying. The world is full of perverts.

"Veeve," drawled Treena in her MTV VJ accent, an unsettling fusion of Swedish and North London streetspeak. "Veeve, have ya revised for that French exam?" In class I pretend I can't be bothered with the language, I am above it. In fact the knowledge that I'm bad at it upsets me because I associate French with beautiful people. The other day I scribbled, with lipstick, on a photograph of Catherine Deneuve.

Treena began to bite around the edges of another finger of chocolate. She looked up from her dark, velvety lashes. She knew, from her mother's experience, that blond eyelashes are ineffectual, and dyed them brown. "I ain't revised."

"That's great, Treena. Because not only have I not revised, I haven't learnt. I have sat in French class for five years, watching Madame turn grey and die in front of my eyes. I have learnt nothing. I can ask myself my date of birth, but I can't reply. I can issue myself with a return train ticket to Dieppe. I can ask at what time the swimming pool opens, and that's it. I'm fucked and I don't want to talk about it."

"That's funny, man. Because I was, like, totally fucked last night. Me and Marcus was out of our fucking heads, man."

"Marcus and I," I corrected her, and went to bang my head on the door of a toilet stall.

*   *   *

On my way home from school I bought a copy of the *NME* because Ray was on the cover in an article by Tommy Belucci.

I read the opening paragraph of Tommy's interview:

> RCA's A and R man only went to see Ray play because he fancied the female drummer in the support band. He failed to pull her, stayed to watch Ray, and the rest is history. It is incredible to think that Ray Devlin's astonishing success story hinges on a girl. A girl!

Tommy Belucci, Ray's best mate and a "crackerjack" music journalist, has a chemical reaction to women. The minute a girl walks into a room, he bristles and sits up dead straight, like he forgot to take the coat hanger out of his suit before putting it on. That's how comfortable the female presence makes him.

The way he deals with his discomfort is to take them to bed. He will say anything to get them there. If they are brunette, he'll say he hates blondes. If they're a blonde, he hates brunettes. If they are studying fashion, then fashion is his single greatest interest in life. His intent is so great that for the next hour, as if by magic, he truly does know everything about the world of couture. If they loathe football, then so does he. If they will only date black men, his skin gets darker. If they like Mel Gibson, his accent becomes Australian. If they fancy Hugh Grant, it turns out Tommy was educated at Eton. Tommy is the Zelig of playboys. I get the feeling he doesn't especially enjoy the sex. The point is that, once he has slept with them, the enemy has been confronted and defused and he will never have to acknowledge their presence again. I'd hate to be him. Life must be one big game of Alien Invaders. Every time he blows up, another comes along.

His eyes are his best feature, brown flecked with green and so heavy lidded there is no crease at all—they are almost Oriental. But instead of deflecting attention from the rest of him, his beautiful eyes just make it worse. Immediately under his eyes are deep, deep bags, the colour of school uniforms. His tiny snout of a nose is much too little for his big face. His eyebrows don't so much meet in the middle as have elaborate and well-catered functions in the centre of his forehead.

Tommy is a mod. He has an extensive collection of Motown 45s and Small Faces rarities. He owns an astonishing array of Savile Row suits and Fred Perry suits. They would be a wiser investment if he just dotted them around his room for everyone to admire because, no matter how well they are cut, they hang badly on him, like clingfilm around a bowl of day-old dog food. He is concurrently thin and lumpy, and elegant suits accentuate this.

Over his suit, he wears a camel-coloured three-quarter-length coat. He doesn't put his arms through it. The coat is draped nonchalantly across his shoulders. So nonchalantly that Superglue is bound to be involved. He carries a briefcase. Like his life, he bought the heavy model to disguise the fact he has nothing in it. Tommy is always pulling things out of his inner coat pocket. Chewing gum, a lighter, a packet of cigarettes, a pen. He pulls them out very slowly, allowing his hand to rest in the pocket like a child patting a bunny. He takes things slowly out of his pocket because he wants us to think it might be a gun. He wants it to be a gun. One day I think it might be, and he'll be so shocked he'll drop it and shoot his own foot off.

Tommy thinks he is in the Mafia. Tommy thinks he is the Don. I'm not sure what he thinks he is the Don of, exactly. The Don of mod. The Don of Small Faces B-sides. If there is, at any point in your conversation with him, a lull or brief silence, he will seize it as an opportunity to talk about his Italian heritage and how he is a son of the Sicilian ghetto and how, even in his flat in Muswell Hill, his homeland stays with him. The only way to shut him up is to hiss, "Tommy, eh? That doesn't sound very Italian. Bloody cold day in Sicily when you were born."

The other thing about Tommy, the least important thing to him and to the rest of us, is that he is a journalist. He is a very poor writer and has, consequently, been at the *New Musical Express* for twenty-three years. He was there when punk hit and, later, when acid house broke. Not that you'd have noticed, lost, as he was, in a desk of dexys. "Speed, man, speed. That's yer ticket. Keeps yer looking sharp. Keeps you alert, so no fucker can get one over on you," he called after the twenty-three-year-old juniors as they headed off to make their names reviewing The Mondays in Manchester. Only moderately talented writers, they lived the raves enthusiastically and got messily luv'd up, but were careful, on the train home, to record their experiences word for word, ensuring fast promotions.

One night, around 1991, Tommy took an Ecstasy tab and, within a few hours, decided he could dig the Madchester groove after all. But the *NME* had moved on to grunge, and the star hacks were flying off to interview the movers and shakers (rather slumpers and whingers) in Seattle and to flirt with heroin. Just enough so Cobain would like them, but not so much that they couldn't get their copy in on time. Tommy, meanwhile, was mixing his speed with his Es and writing like a demon. An illiterate, incoherent demon.

That's the story of his life: Right drugs, wrong time. Right profession, wrong decade. Right clothes, wrong body. When Ray made it big, Tommy was, like a disbelieving wife, the very last to know. Now that he does, no one could know more. That is his way of saving face. Now it is his divine right, he is the official sponsor of Ray, his appointed scribe, his court jester, and no one, not even his boss at the paper, can take that away from him. Not when Ray is so cheerfully complicit in the scam. Tommy never had a pet band before. Or he did, but they were all dead. Or they were alive, but wouldn't let him play with them. Now he has one, Ray's band, Rain, and he won't let go, like those Missouri pit bulls that keep their jaws clamped around your leg even after you've blown their brains out.

Now all Ray's roadies save him a place on the bus when they know he's coming, and when he has no reason to be there, no review to do or interview to conduct, Ray allows him to DJ for him, so he doesn't feel left out. In truth, it is ultimately less humiliating for Tommy to warm up for his idol than to interview him, as the interview usually reads something like this:

Tommy: Are you still a vegetarian, Ray?
Ray: Yes.
Tommy: Yeah, yeah, man. So am I. Killing baby cows.

Bad news, man. So, that girl in your new video, which I watched you film today, she's pretty.

Ray: Very pretty.

Tommy: Very bloody pretty indeed. It was a fun day. Maybe next time I'll even be in the video myself.

Ray: Maybe, Tommy. You're the man. You've got the look.

Tommy: You don't let journalists in, as a band, so I'm privileged to be so close to the heart of Rain. The demos of the new stuff have been unbelievable. Mind-blowing. What's your favourite track on the new album?

Ray: I'd say "Reason to Believe."

Tommy: Amazing song.

Ray: Or "Season to Season."

Tommy: Boss tune, that. Double boss.

When I got home, Manny was under the sunbed. I used to use it but it made me break out. Now I aspire to the pale and interesting, Bride-of-Dracula look. I recently bought a stack of ancient fan magazines from a charity shop and cut out a picture of Elsa Lanchester—the real bride of Dracula—but I couldn't find anywhere to put it. The walls of my bedroom are barely visible for posters and magazine cuttings. They are assigned by decades. Furthest from me are prints of Gloria Swanson, Louise Brooks, and Clara Bow. By the door are glossies of Lauren Bacall, Rosalind Russell, and Cary Grant. Across from that are Marilyn, Marlon, Monty, and Mitchum. The wall nearest my bed has pictures of Albert Finney, Julie Christie, and Terence Stamp. Mod is the most modern that I get. They keep watch on me as I sleep. Treena always asks, Wouldn't you like just one picture of Puff Daddy? But I won't even hear of it. Old people's music. The fact that Manny has enjoyed this stuff, my stuff, is far better assurance than Puff Daddy that I am still young.

I flopped on my futon and rang Ray. You have to let it ring at least ten times because his hearing is not so hot following an amp explosion last summer. Whilst I waited for him to answer, I flicked through the *NME*, pausing on a photo I knew would infuriate him.

Ray's big enemy, although they've barely met, is Dillon from Skyline. Skyline are the biggest band in Britain, even bigger than Ray. He's just one man. They are a whole band. The band have been friends since they were five — playing football together, dodging class together, and forming a band together. Skyline are huge in Europe, and about to make it in the United States. Their name is so big, they *had* to conquer America. Ray Devlin sounds like someone who should conquer part of Cambridge, or Scarborough at most.

Dillon is blond but looks like he should be dark. The *NME* photo showed him in the back of a cab, his arm around a girl with bare legs and sandals that tied all the way up her ankle. He is a walking rat with the scent of Depp. He's rodentine, but if you squint your eyes and think really kind thoughts, you can almost see a touch of Johnny Depp in him. It's only a dab of Depp and it fades the longer you have his poster on your wall.

Not that I would have a Skyline poster. Girls at school do. They are the people's choice. Satellite-television-listing magazines put Skyline on the cover, regardless of whether they have a story inside, simply because they shift issues. Politicians court their support in an attempt to win the Yoof vote. Cabdrivers talk about them. Supermarkets pipe easy-listening versions of their hits down the aisles to encourage you to spend more. Skyline make music to sing in the pub and on the terraces. The verse usually rhymes "do you?" with "what's it to you?" except they pronounce "you" as "ya" because they're from Liverpool. And they say "la" at the end of all their sentences, as in, "What do we think of Ray Devlin? All right if you're a Southern ponce, but he can't touch us, la." The Skyline chorus is always vaguely aspirational: "You've got to . . . Be true to yourself / Believe the dream / Fly higher than the stars." It doesn't matter what. People are always grateful to be told what to do. I'm sure that's the main reason they've sold seven million albums.

Ray's music has more levels. People play the new single and say, "Will you listen to all those levels?" It's very popular with students who get their belly buttons pierced and then take the rings out when they go home to their parents. Skyline's records seem to come out of a pod marked "big sales." Ray is steeped in The Kinks, David Bowie, The Velvet Underground. But because he's so handsome the little kids latched on too. There are never enough levels for Ray. "They just don't get it. They don't deserve to either. I wish I could stand at the counter of Our Price record store and say who could and couldn't buy my music. Not her, she's twelve. Not her, she's wearing a Skyline T-shirt. Not him, he's got dyed green hair."

If he had it his way, Ray would not sell his records to anyone who doesn't love Woody Allen. This is Ray's thing, his safety blanket. He's a Woody Allen freak, talks about him in every interview, thanks him on the sleeve-notes, dedicates songs to him onstage. It's the main thing I hate about Ray— he thinks if he goes on about Woody Allen, everyone will think he's a misunderstood intellectual and that he'll be able to get away with any neurotic behaviour he sees fit to fling at the record company, the fans, his friends and family, cancelling gigs, single releases, and dinner parties because he feels we all expect too much of him.

He keeps asking if I think he should send Woody some of his music and I keep saying no, all Woody likes is jazz and George Gershwin, and Ray says the new single's quite jazzy, and I just shoot him a look. His ideal woman is Mia Farrow, even though Woody has moved on. I so do not look like Mia Farrow, it's not even funny. I don't look like anyone Ray fancies, which is pretty impressive, considering he fancies everyone. Ray says amazing things like "I haven't decided whether or not I fancy Tori Amos." Like Tori Amos is sitting there on tenterhooks, unable to work, waiting for Ray to decide.

He has never, ever made a move on me. He has had plenty of opportunities to swoop on me, in the kitchen of his flat, unchaperoned by Manny.

Four in the morning and Treena was on the doorstep, off her face. As he bustled her into the kitchen, Manny shot me a look that said, "This should not have to be your problem." I was excited that it was my problem, that she had come to me instead of Marcus.

The multitude of drugs Treena had ingested made her eyes even more hypnotic than usual. Her wet clothes clung tight to her long, lean body. Who could blame them? I mused sulkily. Manny left wordlessly to make up the spare bed, a Jeeves with a preference for working-class Spaniards.

Treena was rustling through the biscuit tin. "I came here," she shrieked, "because you always have so much chocolate."

Trust Treena to be the one person on earth whose appetite was intensified by amphetamines. "Keep your voice down, love. It's very late. People are trying to sleep." I was trying to calm her down, a difficult enough task when she was sober. Treena had an entire Mars bar in her mouth. "Spit that out. You're going to choke. Come on, tell me what's happened."

She slid the chunky chocolate from between her lips, cheering, "Look! I'm pooping with my mouth!"

"Oh my God, you're so beautiful and so disgusting."

Finally Treena spat out the Mars bar. "But don't throw it out. I want to save it and eat it later."

I dutifully wrapped up the remains in a napkin.

Suddenly Treena looked tired. "My mum kicked me out." She picked indelicately at her delicate nose.

"Again? Oh, Treena, you're not pregnant? You promised me. You said you'd protect yourself."

"I do!" Treena was outraged. "I make them even when they don't want to. God, you think I'm such a slut."

"You are a slut," I said hopelessly, in a tone usually used to say "I love you."

"Well, maybe, but that's not what happened," she sniffed beguilingly.

I leaned forward and stroked her lustrous, shiny hair. "What, then? What happened? Did she find your stash? Are you going to jail? What happened? You can tell me. It's not to do with Marcus, is it? I won't mind. I only want to help."

The sight of the wrapped Mars bar on the table convinced her and Treena began, testily, to explain.

She shrieked: "I love drugs. I love fucking!"

"Do you really, Trina?" (At this moment I wasn't convinced.)

"No." And with that, she passed out on the sofa.

FOUR

In the end Treena slept with me in my bed.

The next morning, when she should have been choking on her own vomit, she was up and about, even before Manny. She brought me a cappuccino in bed. Even though we've had the cappuccino machine for three years, I still haven't figured out how to use it.

Treena's not clever like me, but she's got it together. She knows how to cook, how to write a report on a book she hasn't read, how to give directions to a Spanish tourist. That's not to say she ever actually does any of these things, but she has the capacity to. Say a terrorist with an Eastern European accent threatened to blow up London unless Treena baked a key lime pie—she would be able to. I see the terrorist as John Malkovich and the pie as delicious.

For months I was tortured by the fear of what would happen if a terrorist, this one from an Islamic splinter organisation, forced me to eat a spider in order to save Israel. I could not do it. I simply could never eat a spider and I carried that shame inside me. My work dropped off, I cried myself to sleep at night, and I snapped at Uncle Manny when he asked me how my day was. Eventually I broke down and told him about my conundrum. He said that, were the situation ever to arise,

I was not to eat the spider because I might go into toxic shock and die. That's my motto now: "Do not eat spiders, even if it will save Israel."

"You're fucking crazy, Veeves," laughs Treena, when I told her about my fear on the way to school. There is no more revolting sound than that of teenage girls swearing on a crowded tube train, stuffing salt-and-vinegar crisps into their cracked mouths between "fucks." I always imagine that that's what they do when they are really between fucks. I see them having unfulfilling, unprotected, acne sex and then rolling away from their odourous inamoratos to feast on savoury snacks, which fill the hole in their soul more successfully than the dick of an eighteen-year-old.

The problem is, I find myself lapsing increasingly into indiscriminate foul language when I'm with Treena, because I can't think of anything to say, anything she'd find interesting. She has the world's shortest attention span and capturing her interest is a very hit-and-miss thing. But if she gets an idea in her head, I have to go with it, or she gets very grumpy and threatens to stop being my friend. Like today, when she decided to count how many freckles I have on my body.

"Oh, fuck off, Treena! You're taking the piss."

"Shut up, it's important. Oh God, Viva, look what you made me do. I've lost my count."

"You're a fucking freak. This is too weird. I can't hold still much longer."

"Wait, I'm nearly finished."

I don't like being inspected that close up. If anyone ever tried to go down on me, I would have them arrested.

We were skipping class, hiding behind the curtains in the assembly hall, counting freckles, when we overheard the headmistress, Miss Hoover, talking to our idiotic English teacher, Miss Danning, about putting on a school production of *West Side Story*. You have to understand our school. It's for daughters of Tory MPs. The only black students are children of Nigerian diplomats. The idea of the girls of Griffins dressing up as Puerto Rican street brawlers was too silly. "They should put on *Flashdance* instead," whispered Treena. We laughed until the curtain shook, then clamped our ears as the click of ill-fitting high heels became louder. I shut my eyes, which is what I always do when I'm afraid, whether I suspect there's a vampire in the bathroom, or a man following me home from school. If I'm going to die, I'd just rather not know. The curtain was ripped back and I heard Miss Hoover growl, "In my office, this instant."

She made Treena wait outside the door while she grilled me.

"Have you anything to say?"

I knew Treena was outside, and even though the door was four inches thick, I felt her spirit in the room and knew that she could hear me. "Yes, Miss Hoover, are you related to J. Edgar?"

"No, I am not," she answered, trying to stay calm, smoothing her fawn nylon pantsuit with a thick, unadorned hand.

"But you like dressing up in women's clothing, don't you?"

"Watch it, Miss Cohen. Nobody likes a smart alec."

"Do you think? I reckon Ben Affleck would have something to say about that."

"I have never heard of Ben Affleck," she hissed.

I raised my eyes from the "It Can Be Done" paperweight on her desk and looked at her properly. Her fringe was trimmed slightly askew, which wouldn't have been so noticeable if all the features on her face weren't so unimpeachably straight. "No, how silly of me. Of course you haven't."

"Viva, you are a very bright girl," she sighed. "You could be top of your class in everything. I know you're keeping your head above water in English and Religious Studies, but that's not good enough. Not for a girl like you. When you joined this school, we had you down as an Oxbridge candidate. Miss Danning gave you a C for your last English essay. You're supposed to be our best English student. You have your English GCSE in just over a month. Why did you only get a C?"

"I got a C because the essay went over her head." Miss Hoover ignored me, despite this being the first truthful remark I'd made in the last half hour.

"Why were you hiding behind the curtains when you should have been in gym?"

"Because Treena's no good at it and I'm too good at it. That's why. What? You asked."

Then Treena was beckoned in. She repeated her conversation with Miss Hoover to me on the way home.

"What are you going to do with your life? What will you do when you have no qualifications and nobody wants to employ you? It's not funny, Katerina, so stop smirking. You haven't stopped to think about what a tough world it is outside the four walls of this institution."

"I have thought about that. If I can't make it by myself,

then I imagine I'll have to marry Donald Trump." She meant it. This was her plan. Easy-peasy. "Of course, I wouldn't want to have sex with him. But one does what one has to."

Miss Hoover informed us both that we had better pull our socks *up* and knuckle *down* for the year-end exams. "Up, down, all around like a seesaw," sang Treena, by way of acknowledgement.

The first exam was on Monday. French. I thought about it over the weekend, even going so far as to buy a new pencil case. In my head, the clean pencil case would make up for whatever I lacked in revision. By Monday morning, I realised that this was not going to be the case.

We never actually said that we weren't going to go to school that day. And we never actually went either. I knew we were missing French. Treena vaguely recollected it once she was reminded.

Treena was relatively restrained for Treena, apart from one heart-stopping moment on the tube when she started cursing loudly that she had forgotten to put on her knickers. She swished her daisy-patterned skirt indignantly as I started talking to my shoes. Otherwise, we didn't talk the whole journey. I studied the tube map. Every stop represented a part of my life I wanted to change.

Covent Garden means the gym I belong to, and the perfect body I have yet to achieve. I have also to achieve actually setting foot in the gym. Piccadilly Circus is Soho. The Coach and Horses, strolling past the sex shops to see if they will try to recruit me. I'd like to be a high-class prostitute who gets paid a lot for doing no more than holding hands. Leicester Square is home to the Boho cinema, where they only show grainy classics. The last thing I saw was *McCabe and Mrs. Miller*. I gazed at Julie Christie as if my very life depended on it. At times, after a particularly bad French lesson, or a row with Treena, it does. "What am I doing here, why am I bunking off school again?" I think, and then sink down very low in my seat so I can stay for the next show.

We got off at Knightsbridge, a stop I usually avoid. We looked like Lady and the Tramp as we made our way to Harrods: the tall, elegant dog, sashaying up the street, turning heads as she went. And the little, scruffy one, skipping along behind her and tripping over its paws. I looked dubiously at the NO JEANS OR RUCKSACKS sign and the ferret-faced doorman. "Why do you wanna come here, Treena? Can't we just go to Camden like usual?"

My voice sounded nasal, as if I had enlarged adenoids. Why was it me whining like a child, after the display Treena had put on last Friday night?

"God, Viva. It's one of the sights of London. I thought you wanted me to be cultured," she muttered as she shimmied in. The doorman tipped his hat and smiled approvingly. I trotted behind her. He put his hat back on. We walked through the lobby, assaulted on either side by girls spraying perfume.

"Aaaagh," breathed Treena, spreading her arms.

"Gross." I stopped, as a squirt of "the delicate new floral fragrance from Chanel" shot straight up my nose, as delicate and floral as the final reel of *Rambo Part 6*.

We ground to a halt at the makeup counter. Rows and rows of lipsticks, pinks and golds, corals, rusts and ambers, vermillions and puce and the deepest, darkest red either of us had ever seen. Except it wasn't called dark red, it was called Petulant Prune. Treena plucked it from between Harlot Scarlett and Aubergine Dream. She tickled the length of the tube until the red wriggled up, like one of those sea creatures you have to coax out of their long, slim shells. "Mmma." She smacked her lips and the lipstick clung on for dear life.

"Let me try that," I said, but Treena wouldn't let me, and gave me Timidly Taupe to fiddle with instead. It camouflaged my mouth entirely. Sometimes I think that's what she really wants. "I'm out of here, Treena," I announced, which I thought carried both gravitas and an air of mall chic. Treena looked over her shoulder at me and made a silent *"Oooh"* through red lips. Then she pocketed five lipsticks and sashayed out of the store. Ahead of me. "Okay, Veeves. We've done commercialism. Let's go hang out with nature."

To me, nature is a really boring accountant whom you don't want to sit next to at a party. I hate parks and trees and fluttering birds of all kinds. And I know whenever Treena's near nature she starts talking about the birds and the bees. "Sex on beaches is no good. Grainy fanny. So not erotic. It's good to be taken up against a tree, though."

Treena then began to relate the tale of her lost virginity.

"Oh, gross, I don't want to hear any more," I shrieked, almost convincingly. "I so do not need to know." Treena was into her stride now, boasting that the guy had never even realised that she was only thirteen.

"Nah," spat Treena. "It was years ago. It didn't hurt as much as having my ears pierced." She paused. "That was really worth it, though."

She told me about her favourite sexual experience.

"So he was taking me from behind."

"From behind what?"

"Behind me."

"Oh. OH."

I couldn't imagine Marcus doing that and I told her so.

"Oh, God no. Marcus doesn't do it with anyone, full stop."

"He doesn't?"

"Hell no. He only wants me. And if he can't have me he doesn't want anyone. He's a good boy. Marcus is a sweetheart. He's the only one I can stand waking up with."

"Not me?"

"Viva! You don't count."

"But Treena"—I looked at her long green eyes and curly blond hair, her wet mouth and honey skin—"Marcus must want to have sex with you."

She stuck her little finger up her nose. "Well, he hasn't tried. He gets what he's given." Still rummaging in her nose, she dangled one shoe from her big toe. "You know, I don't really give a damn about one-night stands. Sex is just sex. It doesn't have to be personal. It usually isn't."

I don't want to have sex for the same reason I don't want to apply for university. What if I don't make it? What if I'm not good enough? Manny's always encouraging me to lose my virginity, telling me that making love is human nature. But if it comes so naturally, why do *Cosmo* and all the other women's magazines carry diagrams of how to do it? The way they write about the female orgasm has led me to believe that it's some kind of exam and you have to do serious revision to pass.

If I had photos of Madonna on my wall, maybe I would be keener to try sex. But I have Liz. And Liz is a frigid sex-bomb. A love goddess who claims to have married every man she slept with. She never did a nude scene because, she scoffed, "Once you've taken off all your clothes, there's nothing left to do but put them back on."

It began to drizzle, and Treena, with her knees curled round the branch and her hair in her eyes, lit a cigarette. The flare of the match cast a shadow across her heart-shaped face that made me wonder if I was safe with her. "What did you do that for?"

The rain was coming down in massive sheets across the park, ridiculously heavy, like the set-up shot in a bad soap opera before someone is murdered. Treena tilted her dirty thoughts to the sky.

We ran across the park. We ran past the stadium. We ran around the lake, where the rain splished sheepishly against the water, in the knowledge that something wasn't quite right, like cousins making love. We unbuckled our shoes and we ripped off our sweaters and we ran with the rain slashing against our bras, dragging one another along.

I arched and leaped, spun and jetéd, and told myself I was the secret love-child of Baryshnikov and Savion Glover. Treena pogoed, a perfectly groomed punk. Her body was so long that it looked faintly ridiculous. A gust of wind tore us apart, slamming me into a bush. I lay panting on the ground as Treena turned cartwheels, then slid on her belly towards me. She rolled beside me, straddled across my tummy, and held my face in her hands, obscuring my view of the over-wrought sky.

"Wasn't that beautiful?" she gasped as if she had just converted to a new religion. "Wasn't that just beautiful?"

I nodded, but the truth is, as we ran I had been terrified

that I was going to tread on glass and that's what kept me moving so fast. I hadn't planned it. I didn't like it. I wasn't ready for my close-up.

Then she kissed me. Her tongue snaked into my mouth. I understood that this was not a gay kiss, just a romantic one. The rain and the park meant a kiss was supposed to happen and I was the only one there. I didn't resent her for it.

We plodded wordlessly back across the park, stooping now and then to pick up a shoe or a sweater. The rain had slowed to a splatter, and by the time we reached the station, had ceased all together. People made way for us on the train. One small boy, glancing at the dripping, mud-stained figures, began to cry. When his mother turned away, Treena made faces at him.

The movie started just as the French exam was ending. I had pulled Treena into the cinema showing the French New Wave festival. I tried to explain to her that it was a different kind of French from the one we're supposed to memorise. You don't learn it, you feel it. You have to understand the eye makeup, as opposed to the verbs.

Treena was engrossed in placing popcorn in the bouffant hairdo of the woman in front without her noticing. She did it very skilfully. "See," she failed to whisper. "I am good at something."

I nodded my head enthusiastically. But she really isn't. She can do things, but that doesn't mean she's good at them.

Last time I was at the flicks was at the repertory cinema, with Ray, for a performance of *Bananas*. It's one of Ray's top seven Woody Allens. I was finding it all quite trying and was only shaken awake by the sight of Sylvester Stallone in an

early role as a subway thug. "Wow! Look, it's Sylvester Stallone!"

Ray slapped his thighs with his hands. "Oh, first of all you
grump all the way through, and then Sylvester Stallone
comes on and it's time to break out the fucking popcorn."

He was angry. I don't even like Sylvester Stallone. I don't
not like him. I just . . . who thinks about Sylvester Stallone? I
tried to explain, "Don't you think it's interesting to see a
young, struggling actor in reference to their current iconic
bubble?"

Ray was just furious, acting as if I had stood up, walked to
the front of the cinema, and started licking the screen. He
doesn't like me making a fuss of anyone more famous than
him in his presence. He thinks it's ungrateful. I know he
wouldn't say it to my face, but in his warped head, he thinks
I'm a namedropper. To him, saying, "Look, there's the young
Sylvester Stallone," is akin to parading outside his flat with a
banner shrieking, "You suck, Ray Devlin, as a celebrity and as
a human being." Treena doesn't mind me "name-dropping,"
because she's never heard of anyone I talk about, not even the
Prime Minister.

After the movie, we fixed ourselves as best we could, using
the hair-drier in the ladies' loo and some of the makeup
Treena stole from Harrods, then we went into Uptown
records on D'Arblay Street, where Marcus was working the
afternoon shift. His hair was braided up on one side and
Afro'd up on the other, and when he saw Treena he started
twirling the three-inch fuzz as if he were Heather Locklear in
a shampoo commercial. Treena went over and gave him a
bear hug. It was so funny because Marcus is this six-foot-four

hardcase, but it was Treena who was doing the bear-hugging, and he crumpled in her arms like Vivien Leigh. Peeping over her shoulder like a baby being winded, he saw me and flashed a Versace smile. Treena didn't let go and, as the music pounded out of the system, she moved him from behind the till and on to the shop front, where they started dancing. Not hip-hop dancing, ballroom dancing. As I said, she can do anything when she feels like it. They looked like they were on wheels.

Jeru the Damaja faded out and "Shame on the Nigger" by the Wu-Tang Clan started playing. Treena reacted as if it were "Boys of Summer." She was still clutching him and he began to come to life like a dying plant spritzed with Baby Bio. I didn't know if it was Treena or the song that was the Bio. They did a weird balldance to "Shame on the Nigger" as it thumped rudely around us. She slipped her feet on top of Marco's orange Air Max Nikes and he wrapped his arms round her slender waist and carried her across the floor. The kids in the store didn't even look up, just kept flicking through the Foxy Brown 12-inches and MC Shaan rarities. I sat on the radiator, watching them dance together, and realised that I was not going to be the only person ever to love her.

Back in Camden we stopped at George and Nikki's for a plate of chips and a coffee. The waiter gave us the coffees for free because he fancied Treena. He handed us two lollipops when we paid him and pointed at a beanie hat on the counter. "See that hat? It belongs to Dillon from Skyline. He left it here when he was with some bird."

I fixed him with a sweet smile as I grabbed the lolly. "I don't care."

But I kind of was interested. I was interested in his hat, in him leaving a little clue.

I made it home with my complexion glowing. Soaked and serene, I sunk deep into the mattress of my bed, turned on the radio, and looked up at my posters for approval. "We love you, Viva," said Ava Gardner. "You don't need school!" spat Paul Newman. "I loved when you did the leap in the park," said Sophia Loren, "and when Treena scared the kid on the subway," giggled Marilyn. I kissed them all and tucked myself in. "Good night, everyone. Sleep tight." But in the half light of my exhaustion, it looked like Liz Taylor was scowling.

FIVE

Ray was smack in the middle of his British tour. He had already been to Liverpool, Manchester, Cardiff, and Glasgow. The venues were medium-sized to large. No mega arenas yet, but 4,000-seaters.

I was planning to see him on this tour anyway, since during the school year he's always moaning about how I'm not interested in his music. I'm not, but I missed him. I missed him whining about how other bands were only doing so well because they appealed to the lowest common denominator, about how much he hated his fans, how he longed to be taken seriously, and how his hair wouldn't do what he wanted it to. He never shut up about Dillon from Skyline. Besides, I didn't want to face Manny's disappointment over the missed French exam.

"Look at his hair. It goes straight back, that's the only reason his stupid band are so popular." Ray looked everywhere for a way to explain the phenomenal success of Skyline and, more specifically, the adoration heaped on Dillon. It was their haircuts, their Adidas sneakers, their Liverpool accents. He could not, for one second, entertain the notion that Skyline were such a big hit because they had unusually catchy songs, and that Dillon was the man of the moment because every-one fancied him.

I decided to meet him in Edinburgh. All the way up on the train, I kept thinking, "Ha! French! It's not even that great a language. So overrated." Listen, see a Chabrol flick and then see an Almodóvar film. Which, excuse me, is the more attractive language? Spanish. Italian is much better. Jesus, French is almost as bad as German. And I hate French film stars. "Oh, I am a pouty French enigma and I like to marry directors twice my age." Fuck off. If you were the evil mastermind behind a plot to blow up Europe, you would definitely blow France up first. I would.

It's a long ride to Edinburgh. I played a game of seeing how long I could make a packet of salt-and-vinegar crisps last. Two hours. You lick both sides of the crisp before you eat it, and when you do, you chew fifty times. It was moderately entertaining. I could see how anorexia might feel rewarding. Although, I'm not really sure anorexia exists. I think it's just a style decision, like bleaching your hair blond. You know there's a risk that your hair will eventually dry and break off, but you happen to think you'll look good very blond, so you do it anyway. I know there must be people who are phobic of eating, who die because of it, but from what I've seen in the school canteen, a large proportion of girls labelled "anorexic" simply went for it because it's cheaper than a pair of Prada loafers.

I found the whole slow-chewing experiment rather Zen, but every time I began to sink into sleep, I was jolted back into life by the yells of the proletariat. There were posses of screeching children running up and down the carriages, so thank God for my Walkman. I listened to Carly Simon and watched the wretched five-year-olds trip on their laces, bawl unenthusiastically, and then wolf down the Smarties their mums bought them from the buffet car. There is something deeply unsettling about a child crying insincerely.

I used to have a nanny from Edinburgh who, any time I said "maybe" in answer to one of her questions, would retort, "Ooh, Mrs. Maybe and her Amazing Baby." I'm a big fan of the Scots. Has there ever been a more perfect face than Sean Connery's? I think not. As I walked through Waverly, I unclipped my hair. It kept my ears warm and, besides, I kept expecting Sean Connery to be waiting, in the newsagents or at the cab rank. I hear he lives in Marbella, but I felt I should look good for him, even if he couldn't see me.

Edinburgh is basically like San Francisco. You always seem to be walking uphill and taxis always cost three pounds—or dollars—no matter where you go in the city. Both are apparently violent cities, with terrible drugs and AIDS problems, but I feel very safe in them. It's always more frightening to read about a terrible crime in a beautiful, tranquil neighbourhood than your average, sleazy crime in your average, sleazy neighbourhood. I suppose the reason so many tourists and au pairs get attacked is that you automatically feel safer away from where you live. In my experience, the closer you come to your own home, the more danger you sense. You know your own bedroom back to front, that's why it's the scariest place in the world.

I could see people bristle when I talked, every hair on their body made static by my clipped London tones, so I didn't ask for directions to anything. I just wandered. There was a market by the National Gallery selling healing crystals and hand-painted T-shirts and I thought of Camden and Treena. I went to the gallery and looked for *Ophelia Drowning*, but she wasn't there. For some reason I thought *Ophelia Drowning* was like a branch of McDonald's—at least one in every major city. The French one would be fancier, the New York one graffitied, and the Beijing one censored, but I assumed she would be there.

I found my way to the hotel to hook up with Ray, but he had already gone to the venue. The man on reception flicked a small, tight smile that told me he had already seen several young girls come up to him and ask to speak to Ray today. I left a note for Ray saying I was there and watched as the man folded it up and put it in his pocket. Pervert. I snuck into the toilets and applied one of the lipsticks that Treena had stolen from Harrods, that I in turn had stolen from her. Bright Red. Red times ten. I kissed the mirror and hailed a taxi to the Playhouse. Three pounds exactly.

By the time I got there, the street was already overflowing with manic pubescents. We're talking nubile fans a-go-go. Scores of girls crowded around the stage door, clad in Miss Selfridge's finest, pale, with legs like plucked chickens. Some were so white they looked blue. Their teeth chattered and goose pimples covered their bare legs. A very few of the girls were so white they looked luminous. The cold made their long hair shine brighter and their hungry eyes sparkle. It was the luminous ones who had backstage passes proudly pinned to their blossoming chests. The passes had the same effect as Baby Bio, and the teenage breasts puffed and swelled under them.

I calmly pushed my way through them and they glared at me, like "Who the hell are you?" The moustachioed security guard stopped me with a weary "Can I help?" and I told them who the hell I was.

"I'm Ray's sister."

The girls looked at me in wonder. The guard just looked at me.

"Are you on the list?"

"No, but that's only because he doesn't know I'm here."

"Sorry, I can't help you, then."

I spoke fast and brittle as panic gripped my lungs. I was in Edinburgh, with nowhere to stay and no one to stay with. "Look, he'll go ballistic if he finds out you've turned me away. I'm his sister." His moustache quivered. I looked around for support. And I realised that I didn't look like the sister of a pop star. I looked like a short girl wearing a lipstick she couldn't carry off, which only accentuated the sad truth: that my skin wasn't luminous enough to merit a backstage pass. I bought a ticket from a tout, who spat a gob of yellow phlegm onto the icy street as he balled up my money. Once I got into the foyer, more security tried to check my pockets, but there was nothing in them, just a ten-pence piece and an empty crisp packet.

Inside the venue, I decided that the best plan was to work my way to the very front of the stage, where he would definitely be able to spot me. He'd get the fright of his life, he'd probably forget his own lyrics, but he'd see me and I would have somewhere to stay. Maybe he'd even make a joke of it and dedicate the next song to his "truanting *compadre*, Viva Cohen," and then everyone would know how special I was. It's weird being in a strange place and having no one to back you up. You could try selling yourself—"Hey, I'm great!"—but the point is, they're not interested. They don't give a damn.

As soon as I swung through the heavy main doors, my wind-nipped ears were assaulted by the most fearful racket since Manny had been told his table at The Ivy was double-booked. This, however, was not a queeny tantrum, but a rock 'n' roll catastrophe, exploding through the auditorium. I could hear a helpless guitar being choked of its life and a bass thwacked soullessly. But there was only one person onstage. I found out, backstage, that it was all made by one machine, a Casio keyboard bought with a kindly aunt's money, and pro-grammed by one man.

I couldn't see that clearly, the hall rendered gloomy by the relentless noise, but I could make out a tiny black-haired boy, all angles and light. He was mouthing words from his mark at the centre of the stage. I could barely hear him, but I could see the sounds creeping, softly, frightened, out of his full mouth, as if they didn't want to leave it. He was so soft, he was almost silent, but all the noise being made onstage clung to his hair and clothes like static and formed a protective laser shield around his little body.

The crowd was indifferent, impatient for the main act to come on. It was booing, throwing bottles, and opting, in droves, for the warmth of the toilets or the overpriced excite-ment of the merchandise stall. And at the stall, above Ray's promotional hooded sweatshirts and moody black-and-white posters, there was a skinny-ribbed T-shirt that spelled out, in gothic letters, the cause of the commotion: THE KINDNESS OF STRANGERS.

This person, the hugely unloved "Kindness of Strangers," was, the merchandising man explained, the "up-and-coming techno-punk outfit" hand-picked by Ray to support him on his British tour. The man, who looked most unamused, handed me a copy of last week's *Melody Maker*. "The Kindness of Strangers—Britain's new existentialist electro-punk genius!" I was unaware that there had been an *old* existentialist electro-punk genius, but I let the subject lie. I wandered towards the stage, dodging the hail of beer cans and blocking my ears, to take a closer look at Ray's new favourite performer.

He looked like he had been separated from his mother and, in the hubbub, somehow ended up onstage. As I reached the foot of the stage, I saw that the little dark-haired boy was, in fact, a young man aged about twenty-two, twenty-three. He was wearing tight, white cord jeans and a homemade T-shirt depicting Vivien Leigh.

His eyes were lined in black kohl and his arms were lined with long, symmetrical cuts, as if someone had started a game of tic-tac-toe on him and then become distracted by the beauty of the board they were playing on. He was pathetically skinny; he couldn't have weighed more than seven stone. When he swept his silky dark hair from his face, I saw he had the most perfect bone structure since the girl on his T-shirt. As the bouncers pulled the plug on the man known as The Kindness of Strangers, dialogue from *A Streetcar Named Desire* crackled onstage.

I was transfixed. He was so thin. He was sooo thin. He had real proper black hair, so black it shone blue. Not many people have that. He was beautiful. The roadies began to clear the stage for Ray's imminent arrival. I hadn't seen Ray play in a few months, but I didn't really want to now. The second the boy crawled offstage, I began to feel unanchored. A few sickly pale girls at the front also seemed agitated. I couldn't quite tell if they were upset that the boy was gone or impatient for Ray to arrive. From their black Miss Haversham clothes, I guessed the former. I went up to a man with a notepad. "Are you a reporter?"

He looked down his John Lennon glasses at me and smoothed his CLASH ON BROADWAY vintage T-shirt. "Yes. I am. From the *NME*." He spoke in sentences punctuated too liberally with full stops, and I knew his writing would be the same.

"What did you think of them?"

"Fucking brilliant. Reminds me of the old days. Clash. Pistols. Stones. Rock 'n' roll as revolution."

"Brilliant." I tried to sound enthusiastic, although, scanning the room and the bottles thrown onstage, I knew this simply wasn't true.

He smiled at me, revealing teeth like a bag of chips. "You're one of the kids. What did you think? Do they match up to your heroes?"

"Um, well, my heroes are dead, so they've already got one up on them."

He laughed approvingly. "Vicious. Hendrix. Cobain? All the greats are dead."

"Um, no. I was thinking more of the dead one out of the Bee Gees."

He stormed off to find some proper teenagers, glaring at me like I was taking the piss. But I wasn't. The Bee Gees are a big favourite of Manny's. My first sentence was inspired by "Night Fever": "Turn the record." I liked The Kindness of Strangers, but, judging by my brush with the *NME*, not for the right reasons. I had to talk to Ray, find out where he'd found this kid, and why he hadn't told me about him.

The lights dimmed. When they came back on, Ray was standing in the middle of the stage dressed in a pair of faded blue jeans with massive turn-ups and a Union Jack T-shirt. I hoped he was being ironic because he looked utterly ridiculous. The crowd was going mental. Girls clutched each other, ripped at their clothes, screamed his name; some even wept. "It's just Ray," I mouthed, who to, I'm not sure, because there I was in Scotland with no friends. I tried to move through the wall of wailers. So undignified. As they clung to the rails at the front, trying to touch his ankles, I grinned up at him. He couldn't see me. The lights blocked his sight lines. I waved and called his name, but that hardly singled me out from anyone else in the room. My T-shirt was biting me under my armpits and my belt was too tight. Sweaty and frustrated, I decided to wait for him backstage.

I grabbed the *NME* man. "Have you got a backstage pass?"

"Yes, I have." He looked down his glasses. "Why?"

I tried another tack. "Is Tommy Belucci here?"

"Yes." Disdainfully, he pointed to Tommy, who was chatting up a girl in a pair of suede hotpants.

I barged between them. "Tommy, can you help me get backstage?"

He didn't say hello, or ask me what I was doing there, say Ray would be thrilled to see me. He put one hand on my shoulder as if he were about to pull me into a kiss and whispered, "Sorry, babes. If Ray wanted you back there, he'd have put you on the list."

I was ready to punch him.

The same moron from outside was guarding the door to the dressing room. I dug my T-shirt out from under my armpits, fluffed my hair up, and tried to look sparkly. "Excuse me, I know we've been through this already, but I really am with Ray. I'm here as a surprise. I've come up to see him. I'm staying with him tonight."

The moron laughed. "In your dreams. Now, if you wait outside after the show, I'll see if I can get an autograph. But if you keep hassling me, you'll have to leave, sweetheart."

I refused to cry. "How dare you. How dare you? Do you value your job"—I tried not to shout—"*sweetheart?*"

He stared at me in disbelief, then moved as if to hit me. "Out. Out right now." He began to march me away. I could hear Ray missing the notes. The guard twisted my arm behind my back, and I felt I might pass out. He wasn't trying to get a surreptitious feel of my bum, either, which really upset me. He held me as if I were one of those little dogs that look like rats. Gangs of girls were staring, laughing through frosted lipstick and hairdos that tickled their faces. I closed my eyes, priming myself to hit the cold concrete. When I opened them I saw the little boy from The Kindness of Strangers. He reached up and tapped the bouncer on the shoulder.

"Hey," he said calmly, "she's with me." The bouncer loosened his grip.

The boy handed me a backstage pass.

"Oh, she your sister, is she?" he huffed.

"Yes," said the boy, "and I haven't seen her for two years so I'm very glad I found her before you threw her out."

I straightened myself. "Thank you."

The boy nodded. "No problem. I can't stand arguments, especially physical ones."

I looked at him oddly as I followed him backstage. He had a dressing room the size of a shed. Inside it, the walls were taped with pictures of Marilyn, Vivien, Audrey, and Elizabeth, and candles flickered around them. It was quite a sight.

The boy touched their paper faces proudly. "I always do that before a show. It's a little ritual."

"I always say good night to them," I gasped, and then, before I could stop myself, "Are you gay at all?"

The boy blushed. "Oh, no." He looked up at me through strands of black hair. "But I'd like to be. I think I could be"— he smiled weakly—"if I tried."

The promoter, huge and red and wearing a Ray Devlin T-shirt, came bursting into the room and started ripping down the pictures.

"No!" cried the boy, throwing his body in front of his girls. "Please, not them."

The promoter crumpled Marilyn, as if she hadn't been crumpled enough in her life. "That," he spat, "was not a full half-hour set, Mr. Electro Genius. That was ten minutes at most. And it was shite."

The angry promoter refused to pay him.

The boy didn't answer, but calmly pulled a Stanley knife from his back pocket and scratched a line down his forearm. Blood trickled down his wrist and the promoter backed off, slamming the door behind him. The boy smiled silently, his mouth curling up at the corners like Salvador Dalí's moustache. Then he walked out of the room, turning at the door to beckon me with him.

He was so thin. I kept coming back to that. When I couldn't focus on anything else, I thought about that. It was my Buddhist chant.

"Do you want to get something to eat?" I heard myself ask.

He shook his head. "But I wouldn't mind a drink."

In the cab to the Thistle, where Ray's record company was paying for my new friend to stay, he told me he was called Andrew or Drew, that his favourite playwright was Tennessee Williams, and that he was unhappy but felt he might be happier under Soviet Communism, and I told him my life story, starting with the Bambi anecdote. I explained that I was a friend of Ray's and explained what I was doing here and that I had missed my French and Biology exams and was missing my English GCSE on Monday. His eyes lit up. "Oh, the French are the fathers of Situationism!" Like he was saying, "Oh goody, pistachio ice cream!"

In the lobby of the hotel I tried Ray's room once again but he wasn't there, or so the girl on reception said. We went to the bar and Drew spilled a bundle of two-pence pieces on the table to pay. He shrugged his shoulders and said, "Shall we take these upstairs?"

I hoped this didn't mean what I thought it did, but then again, I hoped it did. I went with him, probably a little too easily, but I couldn't help it. I tried not to look at myself in the elevator mirror. I wanted him to think I was the sort of girl who didn't care what she looked like, so assured was she of her beauty. I'd picked it up from Treena.

Six

The TV was the first thing he turned on, before the light switch, as if doing so were a safety precaution. We both felt its effects immediately. His tiny, twisted shoulders loosened and he ran his pale fingers through his feathery jet hair. "Technology is the modern comforter," he smiled, patting the television. I was glad it was there and I was not completely alone with this coal-eyed stranger. It was a boxy black-and-white 1950s set with a fat dial instead of a slim remote control. It was as comforting and curious to swallow as a Sunday roast after a week of Japanese noodles.

As Drew twisted it into life, the shabby little room softened and hummed, the protruding nails where no pictures hung melted into the walls, and the raggedy carpet became thick. The whirr from the screen even seemed to block out the cold seeping through the window where the frame didn't touch the pane. The room was a winning combination of crashed-out, drunk-in-the-bathtub rock 'n' roll excess and insomniac librarian's tidiness.

The bedside table was littered with bottles of vodka stuffed with ash and cigarette butts. "How long have you been here, Drew?"

His mouth turned down. "Two nights. There wasn't a lot to do." A pile of Calvin Klein underwear was folded neatly on the bed. Drew looked embarrassed and, scooping them up, started mumbling, "The Jewish people, they excel at everything, even the marketing of knickers."

"How did you know I was Jewish?" I frowned.

This worries me, this looking-Jewish thing. If you're Asian or black, at least you know where you stand and how others see you, you can be 100 percent sure that you're going to be treated differently, rather than just wondering. And unless you're one of the Jackson family, you can't change your skin colour, so passing for a goy is never an option.

I remember gazing, gobsmacked, at an anti-Semitic circular pushed through our door. I was twelve years old, and off school because *Key Largo* was on BBC2 and our video wasn't working. I heard the metallic snap of the letterbox and hurried to look through Manny's mail to see if there was anything that might contain a present for me. Instead, I discovered a misspelt letter, plastered with references to world domination and hooked noses and gas chambers and soap. On the next page the author (who, having gone to all that trouble, had forgotten to sign it) ranted on about "Ghastly Jewish eyes, crafty, shifty, *Evil!*" alongside photocopied pictures of Robert Maxwell and Leona Helmsley.

That was the bit I went back to again and again, even after Manny confiscated it and threw it in the bin. Could you really tell by the eyes? I spent weeks staring into the mirror, trying to detect any hint of evil inherent in my irises. I spent so long pressed against the glass that I started to see it. "I am evil!" I roared at Manny, triumphant. He doesn't understand that growing up Jewish in New York is a lot different from doing it in England.

We need to know if you really can tell, if you can always tell by our eyes and nose and table manners, before some mad skinhead at Finsbury Park station points it out to us: "Oi, big nose! Oi, yiddo!" It happened to my friend Rachel when she was coming back from a party. She's never even been to a synagogue, not once.

It's easy to enjoy being Jewish if you look like Natalie Portman. But what if you look like Harvey Weinstein? Then you can't always get away with it.

I stared at this beautiful bird-boned boy and wondered if he was being anti-Semitic and wondered, most of all: "How did you know?"

"I could tell. You look it. But also, I heard you were. Ray told me all about you. I was telling him about my idea for a Marlon Brando concept album, with each track representing a different film, and he said I should meet his friend Viva, who knows all about every film ever."

Now, any other time, hearing that Ray had said something nice about me would have pricked my interest, but the gossip just bounced past me. I watched it come to rest by the door. I kept an eye on it for the rest of the evening, but I couldn't be bothered to go and pick it up. "Every film ever?" I chuckled. "Not true. I have a Paul Verhoeven gap."

Drew looked disappointed, then, turning the volume on the TV off, exclaimed, "Well, who needs him? He's hardly Billy Wilder, is he?"

"No," I answered slowly, as it hit me just how odd this boy was, "he's an entirely different director."

"I know." He blushed.

"I know you know," and I laughed, pulling a face that was supposed to say "Duh!" but still be pretty. I realised immediately what he was. The boy was a Jew-fancier. I'd never met one so young. How quaint.

Jew-fanciers are gentiles who choose to surround themselves with Jews—befriend them, marry them—and to immerse themselves in Jewish culture. Some go as far as to convert—the sight of Sammy Davis Jr. and his Swedish actress wife, May Britt, lighting the Shabat candles was apparently a sight to behold. Of course, Liz not only married two and converted, but to this day, she practically injects herself with Jewishness.

A white who thinks he is black is called a Cream Nigga. A gentile who thinks he is Jewish is a Me Too Jew. Being a proper Me Too Jew takes more dedication than that imparted by Treena, Tommy Belucci, and all those terrible mod boys who genuinely think they are black merely because they have an exhaustive Motown collection.

With Me Too Jews, the explanation is usually that they just enjoy being different, and take great pride in being outsiders. It's weird. They go on and on about Jews, but they never want to be tailors, violin makers, or Holocaust survivors. They always want to be Arthur Miller.

As he tidied, sweeping up the ash from the case of an Iggy Pop CD, Drew suddenly started burbling again, as if he had been briefly under water, talking away, and, afloat again, was ready to resume his babble.

"Now, everyone knows about Marx and Freud and Einstein, but it's amazing to think you also invented jeans. Levi

Strauss. And boxing, as we know it, was pioneered by Daniel Mendoza. Chocolate, even—the Hershey family."

"They're not Jewish. They should be, but they weren't."

"Not even Barbara?"

"I don't think so."

"Oh." He sat down on the bed, as if faint from shock. I tried to think of something nice to say.

"Well, you know Liz Taylor converted when she married Mike Todd, and had a proper Jewish wedding with Eddie Fisher."

He smiled, wanly. This was a dumb conversation to be having. If Manny'd been there, he'd have been rolling his eyes.

As soon as I thought it, Drew got up and announced, like a ventriloquist's puppet, "You call your uncle whilst I'm in the shower." His timing didn't surprise me because Manny has taught me to believe in telepathy and the power of the mind. ESP is perfectly believable because it is conducted human to human, like a cheaper and more immediate e-mail system.

Manny says everything else is bullshit, especially tarot, because the future isn't fixed. Ghosts come to us at our beds at night, rouse us from our sleep, because all they are is a dream. I sometimes feel someone sitting on my chest and clasping my throat in the middle of the night, but Manny explained that it's just me, holding my breath. Ghosts are a get-out to cover up how powerful our minds and bodies really are. It's less frightening to think that there is a great big bloody phantom trying to choke us than that the stress of everyday living has got to us so much that we choose to hold our breath in the night. That's what he says, anyway.

I believe it. The people I know who enjoy life the most are

the ones who control their own sleep, who decide not to wake up at night, terrified of ghosts, and therefore never do. Treena can be up all night, doing speed, and then decide to sleep, and there she goes. And, no matter how much she's drunk, she can wake up when she wants to. Rather than use an alarm clock, she bangs on her head the time she needs to get up the next day. So if she needs to be awake by eight, she taps her head eight times as it hits the pillow. It never fails.

It struck me that Drew might be a figment of my imagination, an excess of energy generated by my hatred for Tommy Belucci and my fury at the bouncer and Ray, but something about his voice was so unfamiliar, so beyond my realm of celluloid experience, I could never have made it up.

"Drew, if I may ask, where did you get your accent?"

He turned up the volume on the TV and answered, fast and quiet, "It's Middle European."

"It's what?"

"You know, Middle European. Hungarian. Or something."

"Oh my God." I dropped my glass. "Are you trying to do a Jewish accent?"

He ran into the bathroom and closed the door. Oh my God.

Maybe he was like one of those serial killers who are so good at deluding themselves that they become an innocent character who genuinely didn't do it. Four in the morning in solitary confinement they might have doubts. Maybe once at four in the morning Andrew called down to reception for a Coke and accidentally reverted to his real accent, Watford perhaps, until he caught himself. God forbid the part-time bellboy flicking through the *Sun*, returning to page 3 to keep himself awake, God forbid he should hear Drew's real accent.

With some trepidation, I called Manny. The answerphone was on. "Hi, you've reached Manny and Viva. Viva is off galli-vanting across the country with degenerates when she should be revising. Manny has gone to buy the new Barbra Streisand album proclaiming her love for James Brolin."

"He can't be that worried," I reasoned. I cleared my throat and spoke, as fast as I could, before he had a chance to pick up.

"Hi, Manny, it's me. I'm not gallivanting. I'm walking at a measured pace and I'm wearing sensible shoes. I'm getting very important life experience. I can't completely explain over the phone. I'm safe. Trust me on this one. It's a good cause. I love you."

I realised as I hung up that the "I love you" was a bad move. It suggested a gun to my head, a tourniquet at my arm, last rites. Shit. "I'm safe," I whispered, under sleepy, warm-wine breath. The alcohol was starting to hit. Please don't let me be a crappy, girlie drunk.

I didn't quite know what was going to happen, or what was expected of me, but I felt in control. In awe but in charge. He wanted me there to balance himself, I sensed, to hold himself back from the edge of something. I didn't yet know what. He just seemed lonely. The male equivalent of the girl so beauti-ful that no one asks her to dance. I perched on the edge of the bed to watch the end of the soap crackling through the TV. It was some late-night American import. Then I heard the water cut off. "God, please don't make me have to look at him with a tiny towel around his midriff." That's when I realised that I was in love with Drew, this weird, skinny, Jew-fancying freak.

He mustn't do that to me. He mustn't bring sex into this. "If he is wearing a towel," I decided, "I'll look away until he gets the message." But it was worse, so much worse. Drew came out of the bathroom wearing white flannel pyjamas. His hair was tousled. He looked like a freshly laundered bunny rabbit. A fluffy chicken with jet black hair.

He reclined on the bed. The single bed. The only piece of furniture in the whole damn room. Unless I sat on the floor I had to sit on the bed. But I was blocking his sight lines to the TV. Because we had only gone up there to watch TV, I took a deep breath and lay down next to him on the duvet. I sucked in my body so that not one hair on my arm touched his. I even pointed my toes away from his.

"May I take my shoes off?"

"Of course." He giggled.

I was terribly aware that my feet smelled. But it would look too silly to put my boots back on.

"Beatle boots." He pointed at my shoes as he reached for the Vladivar.

"Ah, I s'pose so. I suppose so." Enunciation. He's so big on accents. It matters to someone like him. "They're not supposed to be. I didn't mean them to be."

It is terrible, the things clothes symbolise. You might have short legs and turn your jeans up and people might think it's a fashion statement and you're being pretentious.

Drew watched the TV contentedly, as if it were not an American sitcom so bad it was being shown after midnight, but the finest Austen adaptation. His black eyes seemed to suck up all the light from the screen. The room was getting darker and darker, until only Drew's face was lit up. Traces of eye makeup remained despite his shower. Golden-brown shadow around his eyelids, with grey kohl along the lashes and sweeps of black mascara. He used the makeup to enhance his beauty. "So he must know," I thought, smiling. He knew how pretty he was, so pretty that the straightest of straight Edinburgh lads felt fluttery when they saw him.

He stroked his left arm, which was a mess of cigarette burns, thin white welts, and freshly healed scars. The incision he had made in front of the promoter had crusted over with black blood. His forearm looked like a work of modern art. There was something almost beautiful about it. The beauty of organised chaos. I tried not to look, but I couldn't help it and he didn't seem to mind. He even began to explain the marks as if they were notes in a diary.

"That was after a row with my manager. That was after I read *The Grapes of Wrath* for the first time. That was after I saw *Wings of Desire*. That was the other day when a taxi crashed into the side of my car."

"Why didn't you have a row with the driver?"

"I wanted to. I was furious. But I told you, I don't like confrontations. So I went home and I did this and then I felt a lot better."

The guided tour of his mutilated arm completed, he scratched his nose and gave a running commentary on the next programme.

I couldn't stop looking at his arm. He saw me staring but didn't attempt to cover it.

"Drew, I have to say something. A Jew would never do that to himself. We've been through enough pain without inflicting it on ourselves."

Tears pricked his eyes. "I know everyone thinks I'm Blanche, but I really want to be Stanley," he whispered, and a fat tear trickled down his cheek. I didn't know what to say, or what to do. I reached out to touch his hand, but he flinched like a lizard, like a cold-blooded animal.

I was shocked. "I'm sorry, Drew, I'm not trying to, you know . . . I'm not trying to get off with you. I just wanted to hold your hand, because you look so unhappy."

"I don't like being touched."

"Drew, I promise, I will never touch you."

He smiled and I saw all his teeth.

I felt flustered. I'll go out of the room for a minute, I decided, and when I come back, everything will be fine. I excused myself to go to the toilet. I washed my hands and as I did so I noticed a razor on the side of the sink. It was a ladies' disposable razor. The protective guard had been snapped off and the blade stuck out at an angle. The white plastic stem was dotted with red. What was that in response to? The new dog-food commercial? "All right?" he fluted, as I came back into the bedroom.

I meant to answer, "Yes, I'm all right," but it came out, "You know, Tennessee Williams hated Jews."

"He did?" squealed Drew, genuinely startled.

"Yes, probably. He was from the South. Truman Capote has an evil Jew in *The Grass Harp*. And they were great friends, weren't they?" Drew was on tenterhooks, so I attempted to qualify my statement. "I mean, everyone hates Jews, don't they?"

"I don't," he chimed. "I love them."

I started to laugh uncontrollably, until my tummy felt like

it had thumbtacks in it. But when I raised my head to look at him, I felt strangely calm. I forgot how silly he was. Ray was such a big lunk. Drew was the tiniest man ever to have existed. A waif in sheep's clothing. Oh God, I felt myself turning into Manny. Drew had a blob of excess mascara in the corner of his left eye. I really, really wanted to clean it off. I just wanted him to be perfect. I just didn't want him to have conjunctivitis. And such chipped nail varnish. That's how much he hates himself. He walks around quite happily with chipped nail varnish.

"Do you have any nail polish with you?" My voice sounded very deep and ancient, like I was the chain-smoker. If I couldn't prevent him getting an eye infection, then I was at least going to fix his fingernails.

He hopped off the bed and rummaged in the Hello Kitty makeup bag on the dresser until he found a bottle of ruby red Helena Rubinstein. I winced when I saw it. Winona Horowitz changed her surname to Ryder. You would have thought Helena would have had the good grace to think of a nail-polish stage name. Real old ladies' varnish. But I knew that was why he had chosen it.

I moved his hand to the knee of my black jeans. I saw the terror in his eyes and could see what he was thinking: "Oh shit, she wants me to touch her." I did, but not like that. As I painted his nails I thought that this was probably the happiest I'd been in a long time. With every stroke of varnish, I felt happier and less worried. I admired my neat job and leaned back on the bed.

His thighs were so skinny. Mine spread around me, they seemed to envelope us both. Why does my body have to be so aggressive when I'm feeling so timid? Drew saw no different from the builders on the street. To him, my body was rampant and cheap and therefore I must want to have rampant, cheap sex. Josephine Baker said she had an intelligent body. Mine is so lazy and common and ignorant, as if it has seen nothing but salt-and-vinegar crisps. As if it hadn't been there when I read *Pride and Prejudice* or saw *Taxi Driver*. It only recalled the popcorn I ate in the cinema.

He lit a Marlboro and I looked up at him. He had no five o'clock shadow, just fine, downy hairs on his face that caught the light and made him look even more like Marilyn Monroe in heaven. He was so un-Jewish-looking, I again had to stop myself from laughing. He dragged on his Marlboro. There couldn't be a more inappropriate brand of cigarettes for him to smoke. He wasn't the Marlboro Man. He was the Fairy Liquid baby.

He managed to pull himself off the bed and fumbled again in his Hello Kitty bag. When he came back he handed me a seven-inch record and beamed. "This is my new single."

I didn't especially want to hear it and I was glad there wasn't a record-player in the room. To be honest, I wasn't that keen on his music. It sounded like a bleepy racket. I just liked him. I felt like a studio executive who wanted to shag a starlet without having to put her in his movie. How could I touch him again? In a pre-agreed way. Without, you know, actually touching him. I had to think of a way I could be allowed to touch him. Maybe if I said that it was Jewish law. I daren't ask to paint his toenails. Maybe he would be too drunk to notice. So, holding my breath, I awkwardly began to stroke his hair and ask a lot of dumb questions.

"Is your hair the same colour as mine, really?" If it was, this would give us something in common and he would have to love me. If his hair was an entirely different colour, he could comment on the loveliness of my hair and wish his was the same colour as mine.

His nose was in his vodka. He snorted, by way of reply. Perhaps he couldn't bring himself to say I love you.

"I'm just quite a touchy-feely person," I apologised, and he sniffed, "I noticed," sounding for one second like one of those terrible, cruel girls at school. Then he spun around and stared dramatically at me, as best he could through his snow-drift vodka haze.

"What hope do you hold for your sex?"

He saw the horror on my face and realised he had said "sex." I could see he had an even stronger abhorrence of sex than I do. "Gender, gender," he corrected himself. "What hope do you hold for your gender?" As if that were any less of a stupid question to be asking at three in the morning.

I took a deep breath. "I think things will get better." This did not sound like an answer as important as he seemed to think the question was. I thought quickly and added, "Women are better than men."

He nodded his head enthusiastically, then closed his eyes, relishing the truth. Not only was he not Jewish, but also the gender he belonged to was, indeed, inferior.

I should have been thinking, "What a jerk," but all I thought was, "Baby doll. Poor, sweet, exploited baby doll." I decided there and then I would protect him from modern society. Or from horrible groupies anyway. Idiot words kept coming out of my mouth. There was so much I wanted to ask him, but he couldn't talk anymore. His eyes were glazed, his head lolled.

I had to be strong and leave. I could not be there the next morning or he might not remember that nothing had happened. I told him, "I'm going now. Thank you for having me," like it was a goddamn children's party and he was going to give me a going-home present. I slowly did up the buttons on my jacket and heard myself ask, "Can I give you a hug?" He consented and I threw my arms around him. I was careful that my breasts didn't touch him but surprised myself by kissing his neck. He wouldn't remember. I left him lying on the bed, swathed in smoke, ashtray on his groin, ash overflowing onto his white pyjama bottoms.

It was 5 A.M. and I was on the streets of Edinburgh by myself. It was the third day of June, but I was so cold that if I hadn't been so drunk, I would have sat down on the pavement and cried. When I left the hotel, there were still girls sitting in the lobby, waiting to meet Ray. They had been there all night, at first sitting up straight and looking chatty, trying simultaneously to seem engrossed in their conversation and keep a nervous eye on the door for when Ray did make his entrance.

After an hour of listening to each other with fixed smiles and talking without speaking because they were so excited, they started to take turns going to the bar. Now they were so drunk their legs were sprawled rudely to either side of their chairs and their coats lay on the floor. First impressions count, especially at dawn, so they had on just their jeans and tiny little T-shirts that tugged under their armpits and stretched taut across their breasts. The cotton was splashed with red wine, so, with all of them collapsed with their eyes heavy, it looked like there had been a hotel massacre. The breasts were elegant and neat, but the T-shirts were slutty. The balance was, I calculated, pretty much on the mark, and if Ray had been there, he would have taken any of the lovely nubiles to bed.

I felt so much older than them.

On the train back from Edinburgh I didn't have to entertain myself by seeing how long it can take to eat a bag of crisps, because I had a photo of Drew to look at. It was from a fanzine I found in a record store off Princes Street. To be in the music business for only two months and already have your own fanzine! There it was, beyond the Ska and Goth sections, displayed *above* the Morrissey and Nick Cave tomes.

The picture was photocopied, smudgy black-and-white — but that was a fair enough description of how he looked in real life. Blissfully two-dimensional. Whereas someone like Ray spends his days trying to prove how multilayered his life is, Drew was more than happy to be a cartoon. This fanzine was called *Stellaaa!* and featured a profile of Montgomery Clift, a critique of Edgar Allen Poe's "The Pit and the Pendulum," and a drawing of Drew by one fan's six-year-old cousin.

I was seated in the opposite direction from where the train was headed. Ordinarily I would have kicked up a fuss, stamped my little foot, threatened to report the guard to my dad, who owns British Rail. But it didn't matter now. I felt like I was being carried in the right direction. Pulled gently out to sea by a lovely undertow that did all the work for me. It swept me under the water in the stroke of a ballerina's slender arm. And now I was floating between the sea and the surf, I found myself breathing properly for the first time in my life. I considered how constricted my chest felt when I was with Treena or Ray. No more decisions. I talked to Drew under the waves.

"I wish I could cram you inside my mouth, keep you behind my tongue, hide you in my cheeks until I looked like Lionel Richie. Keep you safe. Keep us both safe. You might slowly disintegrate, but at least you would still be in me. I wouldn't feel guilty and try to push the taste of you down with crisps, chocolate, Marmite on toast. I would never eat again. I would become slim and then thin and then skinny and then I would dye my hair black and cut my arms. And I would be so happy."

I was so happy. A fat, runny-faced family across the way smiled at me sympathetically. They were so ugly and it was all so perfect.

I had called Ray from the station to tell him I had been and that I was leaving. A girl answered and passed him over. I deliberately only put ten pence in the phone so the pips would sound before he had time to ball me out. I rang Manny to elaborate on the "I'm safe" shocker. He then rang Ray and yelled, which pleased me no end.

"It's a mercy she met this boy, since your security guards wouldn't let her see you. Rather heavy-handed, don't you think? Turning into Aerosmith, are we?" I know what Ray was thinking, but he didn't say it: that if he had been Aerosmith, the security guards would have let me backstage in an instant, since I had begun to look, quite frankly, like a rock chick. Had Manny noticed I'd gone up a cup size in the last month? Ray had. He found it irritating, I could tell. There he was, trying to act like a kindly uncle, and my breasts kept getting in the way.

Instead he said, "Manny. Do you not think she should have called *before* she came up? Do you not think she should have been in school? And I don't like the idea of her becoming too close to that Kindness of Strangers weirdo."

I took this up with Ray.

"If he's so weird, how come you asked him to support you? How come you didn't tell me about him?"

"I don't tell you everything. He's just a support act. I don't think he's that good."

"Then why is he on tour with you?"

Ray sighed, as if I were a particularly dense fan hounding him for an autograph. "Publicity. I knew a pretentious little art-school kid like him would impress the serious musos."

Manny was so thrilled to see me back in one piece, he forgave me everything. "The school is furious and so am I. They doubt you can re-sit those exams. You'll have to get straight A's in every other subject if you want to stay on for A-levels with Griffins. Darling, Viva, you do look beautiful."

I grinned. "It's catching."

All day long I was the Queen of Sheba. I bathed for an hour and a half, plucked my eyebrows, did a face-mask with Manny, painted my toenails. And then I did my homework. I could do my exams if they were for him. Next up was Maths. Maths, so honest and pure, only one answer to everything.

Ray called me from a Newcastle hotel room in a strop. If the call was to apologise for the Edinburgh fiasco, he was doing a very good job of not letting on. He had gained weight, he moaned. I couldn't stop myself from extolling the virtues of Andrew's tiny waist.

"Really, most men that thin look gaunt, but Drew is just so perfect."

"Huh," said Ray. "I have to go."

When Ray got back to London, he tried to make amends by pretending to get excited about my birthday, which wasn't for another six months anyway. Treena rang and wanted to go clubbing. She always wanted to go clubbing. But I knew how the evening would unfold:

Treena forces me to wear something I'm not comfortable in, something meant for a tall person, but I'll want to wear it because it's hers. She'll look amazing. We'll go to the club, which will, for one night only, be populated by an assortment of scary old men and scary teenage yardies with gold teeth. I will spend most of the time in the toilets, trying to soothe my smoke-stained eyeballs with damp tissue. Treena will get out of her mind on snakebite, snog a yardie, lose her purse, and then we'll have to walk home, hiding behind cars from Treena's new admirer. No thank you.

A prebirthday celebration with Ray, on the other hand. Now, there's a depressing thought. He'll probably give me a copy of *Take the Money and Run* and say, "This was my favourite movie when I was your age." Just as he did last year. Then he'll get maudlin because he's not a teenager and I am. And the more miserable he becomes, the less I'll relish being young because I know for sure I'm going to be like Ray in a few years. Getting to twenty-four and pretending to be really old because the alternative—being an in-between age, neither young nor old—is just too scary.

I wished he could just leave it alone.

"Ray, it's in six months. Nobody cares, least of all me."

"But eighteen, that's a serious one."

"Look, I don't want to celebrate my birthday. Drew says with every year we just get sadder."

"Drew lives in a tree."

"He does not."

On the other end of the phone, Ray began angrily to tie back his hair, tugging until the elastic band snapped. "When are people going to realise that madness and suicide are not synonymous with glamour?" he growled. "The only difference with your Drews and your Kurts is that they are the people who go through the door, while the rest of us stand in the corner, looking at it. It doesn't make them better. It doesn't make them braver. It just means . . . they have a shorter attention span."

I snorted disdainfully. "Look who's talking. You're just jealous because he hates himself more than you do."

Ray slammed the plate of pasta he was picking at to the floor, which was a wasted gesture since those Sharper Image video phones never really took off and, therefore, I could not see him. "Don't be such a fucking teenager. Don't fall for it."

"Look at you. You are so full of rage. Drew is just full of sadness. It wastes him away."

"Are you saying I'm fat?"

"No."

"Drew doesn't give a fuck about you. He's only interested in himself. I'm on tour with the cunt, I know. Did he ever ask you one single question about yourself? Did he want to know about what makes you unhappy? He doesn't know you exist. No fucking talent, no fucking hope. Poncey fucking band that's never going to get anywhere. He's full of shit."

"I know he doesn't know I exist. I know he doesn't care. I know I've made him into this great thing and he's never going to be a success and he's never going to amount to nothing. I know I believe in nothing." I looked at Marilyn, Monty, Marlon. "But it is MY nothing."

SEVEN

Drew hasn't called to tell me his schedule. I didn't expect him to. He's far too delicate a person to deal in telephones. I only gave him my number to show he had a confidante. It's not as if he asked for it. So I found his London date in the *NME* listings page. He was playing some godforsaken hellhole off Charing Cross Road, but I dragged Treena along for protection. She seemed bored, which pleased me. As I said, I only wanted her for protection. I didn't want her to like *him*. I knew he wouldn't like her.

The English GCSE had gone okay. My hand killed at the end, which is always a good sign. It didn't hurt in Maths—I took one look at the paper and excused myself because I was going to be sick. Classics was great. I wrote a fantastic composition about Dido and Aeneas, saying that more lovers should kill themselves on funeral pyres and then there wouldn't be such a high divorce rate. And I think I did all right in History. I was unprepared for questions about Germany's "golden years" of the 1920s, so I wrote an essay about "Golden Years" by David Bowie instead, managing, skilfully, I thought, to link it to the Weimar Republic.

I deserved a night out. Ray was loitering at the bar. Drew was as beautiful as I remembered, only this time his eye makeup was silver and he was wearing a Marilyn Monroe T-shirt. The sound was as irritating as I remembered too, tinny and noisy at the same time. How could such a deep man make such hollow music? I blocked it out and just watched him, going over everything we had talked about in Edinburgh.

He told me that he never had a headache. If his brain ever throbbed, it was because he was suffering a particularly acute attack of twentieth-century malaise, or so he said. In reality, his frequent migraines were a side effect of the anorexia he had been calmly cultivating since the age of fifteen. Although he had the utmost respect for fat people, believing they symbolised the desire for spiritual cushioning prevalent in modern society, he felt thinness was his duty. So half an unbuttered potato was cut into quarters and made to last until five and then he would start drinking—vodka, neat, so as not to have the unwanted calories involved in orange juice, lime cordial, or cranberry. No social drinking, he drank to get drunk. He drank in his bedroom until he felt sleep spreading through his veins. If that didn't work, which it didn't lately, he'd have a joint. He very much wanted to be a heroin addict. It seemed like a shiny drug, a romantic drug. He hated himself for smoking dope, so middle-class, so Sussex University, but he found it was the only thing that sent him to sleep. "Off to beddy-byes," he'd say, turning his back on the party and walking upstairs.

In his room, he'd brush his teeth, tone and moisturise, and unwrap the polythene bag. He wasn't very good at rolling joints. He was not very good at making things work: washing machines, answerphones, his guitar. He took his washing home to his mum, left the phone mostly off the hook, and allowed the technician to do almost all the computer programming in the studio. Although I wasn't supposed to repeat that part. Lately he had taken to chewing the hash whole: foul as it was, at least there was no smoke and no rolling. It pleased him—it felt like taking medicine.

With the sound blocked out, I was enraptured by The Kindness of Strangers' London debut. So were several other girls in the packed pub back-room. I say girls, but they were more women. Too old to get away with ripped fishnets and dyed black hair. And they didn't get away with it. Drew eyed them with ill-disguised distaste. No, no, this was quite the wrong audience for him. These doomed romantics who display all their hurt and isolation through their dress sense. Too literal. And they looked unclean. Drew definitely deserves a better class of hanger-on, I told myself. I see him with Joan Baez. Who he hasn't heard of. He blushed puce when he admitted this and I told him it was no big deal, most people his age didn't know who she is, and he started muttering, "Gaps, gaps, too many gaps," and yanking at his hair.

Ray smoked furiously, tutting softly as Drew sang and then clapping far too loud when he stopped. Treena didn't think much of the show. She referred to Drew as that "weird boy that looks like a girl." I suspect she didn't like him because he was prettier than her. I knew Drew wouldn't fancy her. He liked the type consumed by their appearance, knocked sideways, unable to function because of their snake hips, colt legs, and doe eyes. He liked someone to compete with, and Treena has child-bearing hips with clearly no capacity for anorexia.

That night in Edinburgh, he had told me he enjoyed my face. Something around my eyes suggested the suffering of concentration camp victims, he had decided. Later, on the train home, I realised I had never been so offended in my life. But there and then, I thought, "What a sweet thing to say. He likes my face. How generous." I knew my body terrified him, made him feel physically sick. I could see it—every time I moved towards him, he wanted to scream.

For a while now, I've been trying to compile the definitive list of the ten best-looking people of all time. At twelve-twenty that day, it read like this:

> Yul Brynner
> Elizabeth Taylor
> Simone Signoret
> Monica Vitti
> Claudia Cardinale
> Anne Bancroft
> Harry Belafonte
> Paul Newman
> Sophia Loren
> Drew

You'll notice there's a high Italian female count. Anne Bancroft's real name is Anna Maria Louise Italiano. She changed it when she went to Hollywood because she didn't want to be perceived as just another lusty Italian wench. Now everyone thinks she's Jewish. Simone Signoret was, and I've had big rows with Manny about Paul Newman. Whenever I raise the subject, he practically rips his hair out. "How many times do I have to tell you? Newman is a *Catholic* name." I really, really want Paul Newman to be Jewish, just like Manny really, really wants people he likes to be gay. There just aren't that many Jewish sex symbols and I'm trying to help out. I know, Lauren Bacall, Kirk Douglas, Tony Curtis, although I don't really rate him. Not enough.

I'm incredibly envious of the Italian broads because . . . well, Jews are pretty good, but Italians are even better. Can you imagine being an Italian Jew? I think I might explode with joy. And if you're Jewish, you're close enough that boys sometimes say, "Hey, are you Italian?" and I say, "No, I'm Jewish," and they deflate, like "Oh, why has this image of Sophia Loren suddenly turned into Joan Rivers?"

I'd shown Ray the list because I knew it would annoy him. I knew it would have two effects—to make him feel like the white trash he is (Ray thinks liking Michelle Pfeiffer is the height of sophistication) and to make him jealous with the inclusion of Drew.

"Junkie poof!" Ray exclaimed, as if he were a football commentator, and that were Drew's number. To my disappointment, he would not be further drawn. Instead he initiated a discussion about who had the best chest, Yul Brynner or Paul Newman. We decided it was Yul Brynner. Ray had on a dressing gown at the time, chest casually exposed, and I wasn't sure if I was supposed to say, "Wow, Ray. You beat them all."

I wanted to discuss my list with Drew and I waited patiently for the fishnet brigade to give up and go home. Drew wouldn't acknowledge Ray until Ray stepped right up and slapped him, hard, on the back, at which point Drew stretched out a skinny hand and said, "Hello, Ray, how very nice of you to come," like an etiquette school graduate.

"C'mon, gal," Ray barked at me, "I'll drop you home."

"Uh, no thank you, Ray, I'm going to get a taxi. A little later."

Ray put his arm across my back and let it rest on my hip. "Really, gal. You've got to be up for school."

I was mortified. The way he put his arm round me. It had so little to do with affection and so much to do with property. It was hideous. I was terrified Drew would think we were sleeping together. The way he just rested himself on me looked like "I have her. I might have her again, if I want." I was furious. No way would I let him drive me home. Besides, Ray's car is the most disgusting thing on earth. It is always overflowing with crisp packets and stinks of cigarette ash. Ray is a pig.

The first time he took me out to dinner he ate my dessert when I excused myself to go to the ladies'. I returned to the table to find my plate smeared with the remnants of chocolate fudge cake. This annoyed me because I had repeatedly offered him a bite and he had repeatedly replied, "Oh, no," as if saying, "Oh, no, I don't touch hard drugs." As I sat down, he began to sweep up the crumbs with a wet finger. One morsel of chocolate slipped off his forefinger and made a valiant Steve McQueen–style attempt to escape. In my mind, I willed it onto a tiny motorbike, to leap over Ray's stubby thumb. But he grabbed it and stuffed it between his lips, which were twisted with success.

"Yes, I ate it all."

"You ate it all," I said sadly.

He repeated himself. "Yes, I ate it all."

I was determined that Ray was not going to win this time.

"Look, why don't you drop Treena. She wants to go home."

"Cool," said Treena, skipping out towards the car. Ray ground a cigarette into the floor with his boot and then followed Treena out, not saying another word. I tapped Drew on the shoulder and asked if he wanted a drink. He jumped a bit when I touched him and then backed out of the room, facing me, as you're supposed to do when being menaced by a shark.

"Thank you, Viva, but no thank you. I've got a fanzine interview to do." He motioned to a tall, scraggly seventeen-year-old girl with pale blond hair and watery blue eyes. She didn't look Jewish, that's for sure.

"Well, should I wait for you?"

He smiled with two muscles. You're supposed to use eight. "I'm a little tired." The girl tugged at his arm. He didn't flinch. He must have been very drunk.

"Oh, okay. Well, I'll see you soon." But I knew I wouldn't.

EIGHT

When I think about Drew, I feel so alive that I want to die. His hair, his skin, his cuts. It hits me like a blast of hyperlife. It knocks me sideways so I can't get up. I am six, learning to roller-skate, falling on my coccyx again and again. But it's worth it for the five seconds I'm on wheels, not holding on to the railings, my pink ra-ra skirt blowing above my waist, kneepads strapped to my black leggings. I always fall over just as the mad old man from the next street turns the corner. My body is throbbing with the pain of concrete on butt and the mad old man is whispering obscenities right up close against my ear. I can smell the cabbage and scotch and pornographic magazines oozing from his pores. I can't get up. I can't get away. I can't tell Manny.

I have to stay in bed with a satin eye-mask on my head and eat white grapes with the skin peeled off. I don't think Drew would eat the skin, although I'm not sure. I am certain he pulls the string off the banana flesh before biting it and spits the pips out of apples and folds them neatly in a tissue. I can't stand people who eat apple cores. It's like saying, "Hi! I'm just too much. I will eat your head if you let me."

If he partakes in chocolate, it would be Kit Kats, which are a great favourite of the neurotically inclined: you not only have the four chocolate walls to bite off per finger, but also four individual wafer layers, which you can pull apart like an airline drink mat if you're very skilful. I like Smarties. When I was little, I liked to arrange them in patterns around the toilet seat for Manny to find. And he was always very appreciative and made a big fuss about how artistic and talented I was and how I was going to be the next director of the Metropolitan Museum of Art. When I became director, we would be moved to New York and we would buy back the old family house in Brooklyn plus an apartment in Manhattan, probably a TriBeCa loft next door to Robert De Niro. I bet Drew's favourite Smartie is the yellow one. If you like Sartre, you'd like the yellow one. I just get that impression.

I sense he might have a penchant for olives. His breath is ever so slightly metallic and jagged. If you drink that much, you only have time for bar snacks: mini-pretzels and stale crisps and olives. People who eat olives, who actually like them, are by nature perverse. Because olives do not taste nice. They make you gag the first, second, third, and fourth time you try them. You really have to work at it to start liking them. You have to like pain. Really like it. Because the acrid oil lines your palate for days. Even when you brush it away, the taste comes back to haunt you on those hot, restless nights spent kicking one leg over the sheet and folding your arms under the pillow.

Drew savours unpleasantness, unhappiness, and discomfort like a sucking sweet you take to combat nausea on long car journeys. It keeps him going, stops his stomach flipping over. If you are always miserable, at least you know where you stand. My problem is when I'm happy, I'm too happy. I'm clutching the string of a helium balloon. Manny's crying, "Jump, jump!" but I never do because I have no sense of distance. I can't see how high off the ground I am and what a long way down the real world is. I wouldn't say that my emotions are extreme. I'd say they are committed. My moods are the equivalent of Madonna's dancing: inappropriate but all-out. If I'm going to be sad, I might as well be the saddest a girl can get. And if I'm happy, I want to be the happiest. The trouble is, I feel highs so ecstatic that just being normal feels like a thousand-mile drop and being unhappy is excruciating.

See, I was talking about Drew and now I'm talking about me. Manny says I obsess on other people because I don't want to focus on myself. But in the end, all my crushes come back to me. All roads lead to Viva.

I like the fact that Drew only drinks vodka. True, it is the choice of the alcoholic. But that's good. It means Drew is drinking for nobody except himself. Vodka is the most honest and workmanlike of alcohols. It is there to make you drunk. It does not taste nice. It does not come in a fancy bottle or in an appealing colour. It holds no appeal for aficionados of smelly cheese and fine wines. There is no such thing as a vodka-tasting party. It is clean and see-through and straight to the point.

I can't stop thinking about him. I can't stop relating every situation to him because I know he'd have the definitive view on every situation. Taking the rubbish out is symbolic of the human condition. Watching Australian soaps is symbolic of the human condition. Brushing your teeth is symbolic of the human condition. Have I said that his hair is in really great condition? I've never met a man with such soft hair. Like a chinchilla. Snakes are really very soft and nice to feel too. I guess that's why they flinch. Because they've got to protect their reputation. Otherwise everybody would be coming up and trying to pet them and their skin would probably go all thin from people rubbing their dirty fingers on it. It's like those signs in art galleries: "Please do not touch the sculpture. Even if your hands are very clean you can still damage the bronze." Drew can see the dirt that no one else can see, not even on their own bodies.

I've found that if I do go to school, thoughts of Drew usually come during a Maths lesson.

If I stay at home, under the covers, it happens more slowly, more pleasantly, descending like a fog, like a soothing aromatherapy steam bath. I feel pampered and slightly embarrassed. Manny knocks on the door and I promise I'll get up in a minute. Manny thinks I'm masturbating. I'm not. I never do. My attention span isn't long enough. Treena told me, "You do this and keep doing it until you *have* to keep doing it." No household object is safe from her: cucumbers, hairbrush handles, deodorants. I hope she never wins an Oscar. And she goes on and on about it, which is one of the times with her I just have to switch off.

"Try it again, Viva. Try it for longer." It sounds too much like learning to use tampons. I just think, how stupid. I can't even listen to my favourite two-and-a-half-minute pop song all the way to the end without having to fast-forward. I'm never going to have the patience to have an orgasm. To say, there, no there, up a bit, faster, softer. Here's the bottom line about masturbation: sex must be humiliating enough as it is. But to make all those faces and all those noises by yourself . . . how inelegant.

I wonder how Drew will die? He might pierce his heart with a long knife and then collapse on a pre-readied funeral pyre. For me, I don't mind death, I just don't like the idea of pain. I would take pills, one by one, savouring them like M&M's. I love the taste of Ibuprofen, but I don't know how long it needs to take hold, so I would have my letter written the night before and I would have clean hair and shaved legs. I would lay myself on my bed, with arms folded across my chest, holding in my left hand the list of songs I want played at my service, the photo of me I want to adorn the programme, and the people I want at my funeral. Everyone who had not invited me to their parties at junior school would be invited and made to sit at the front.

Drew would be so struck by my death that he would write a concept album about the little girl, too good for this world, who so touched and inspired him. The girl on the cover would look like me but better. It would sell seventeen million copies. T-shirts with BETTER-ME on the front would be freely available at Kensington Market and Camden Lock. Not so much an album, more a cultural phenomenon.

But I wouldn't kill myself. If I did, I wouldn't be able to think about killing myself anymore. And I wouldn't be able to think about Drew. Part of me says that if I did it, he wouldn't be that impressed anyway. He'd just be jealous that I beat him to it. He might think I stole his idea. Everyone always thinks I'm stealing their ideas. When I sit next to Treena in class, she always covers her tests with her arm, even though all she's done so far is write down her name.

*   *   *

The Maths teacher asks me again: "What is the answer to number twenty-three?" I had completely forgotten the question by now. She writes it on the blackboard. The squeak of the chalk makes me gag. I look at the snail-trail of white powder dotted across the board, but all I see are Drew's cuts beginning to come undone. The scars that were starting to heal turn purple, then blossom into red, like an atmospheric David Lean shot of a flower.

But before the shot has come fully into focus, David Lean dies and David Cronenberg takes over. The dried blood is splitting and coming off in lumps. The wounds are opening, wider and wider. I can see the flesh inside his wrists. The blood pumps out and sprays across the room, splashing the teacher's blouse and making it stick to her breasts. The blood renders the *faux* cream silk a translucent pink and I can see her nipples. The fact that I can see my Maths teacher's nipples distracts me, momentarily, from the carnage in the classroom.

The teacher asks again. "Why are the rest of the class on number twenty-three and you're only on number three?"

I sigh and throw down my Biro. "Because they're good at Maths and I'm not." The blood is gone. I see the question in front of me. It is a dumb question.

At lunchtime I stumble down the hallway to the canteen, where Treena is waiting for me. Girls sit as far away from her as possible. She is chewing tuna casserole with her mouth open. The girls at Griffins have enough of a food phobia as it is without Treena making it appear even more disgusting. When she sees me, she sticks her tongue out, displaying, on the end of the puce muscle, a lump of filo pastry and fish. At the next table Cassie Souter is making exaggerated and compulsive chewing motions with her mouth. There is nothing actually in her mouth. She is chewing her own spit to fool her stomach into thinking she has eaten and is therefore not hungry. She weighs six stone.

Treena is cruel to the anorexics. When she first arrived at the school, she gawped at the walking skeletons whose faces were so thin, the skin stretched across their bones like clingfilm. She stared in a caring way. But now the milk of human kindness has turned sour, and Treena likes nothing better than to taunt a food phobic. "Cassie. Hey, Cassie, I can't finish my lunch. Do you want it?"

"Treena," I snap. She's being mean. If I expressed my twentieth-century malaise by not eating Kit Kats rather than eating Kit Kats, it would be me she was picking on.

"Why? What? She's making me feel sick. She looks like a freak. And the bulimics. My God, their breath stinks! That constant vomiting. It's disgusting. Why should I have to look at those freaks? It's not exactly a pleasant environment to work in. Jesus, my mum took me out of state school because there was always rain coming through the ceiling onto the table I shared with twenty other people. But that's a lot less distracting than Karen Carpenter over there."

I myself can't stop watching. It's like a late-night horror film. Treena's always egging me on, forcing me to look. "Oh my God, Viva, you've got to see. She's lost at least another five pounds. *Look!*" And we both look, and the poor girl feels our eyes, hot with incredulity, burning into her already scorched flesh, and thinks we're staring because she is so grotesquely fat.

Mr. Edwards, the only young, male, and handsome teacher

in our school, is on lunch duty, holding a bell that he has to ring between sittings, to let the young ones know their time is up, that that's all the tuna casserole they'll be having today. A man ringing a small bell basically looks stupid. You can't not look dumb. It's like there's no cool way of pronouncing "banana." It's just a dopey word. Even Mick Jagger couldn't sing the word "banana" and make it sound funky. Mr. Edwards is clutching this little bell, but trying to hold it in a saucy, aloof way, like "Oh look, there's a bell in my hand. Oh look, I'm a teacher in a girls' school. What am I doing here? How odd."

He is flirting with some long third-formers. Their hair is long, their limbs are long, their faces are long. These girls go on forever. I get bored just looking at them. They make me feel like a tiny, tiny, MTV news-update sound bite. Mr. Edwards looks uncomfortable when he sees Treena and stops chatting and starts pacing the dining room, nervously ringing his handbell, like some kind of Humbert Humbert town crier: "Young girls, young girls. And yet more young girls. No more news."

Treena holds the swing door open for me with her foot, spitting over her shoulder at the Knights of the Emaciated Table. "Pah. Lightweights." God, I love her. She truly makes school bearable. If she weren't at Griffins, I would be the most special person there, and it would simply be too much of a burden for me to carry.

If she ever has an off-day, I love her twice as hard, willing her simmering specialness to spark into flame. When she's really hungover and useless, it takes a lot of enthusiasm on my part to get her kicking again, but I'd rather expend energy that way than spend the day feeling odd because Treena isn't as good as she's supposed to be. I feel very alone with my love. It is the kind of love that needs nothing in return. In fact, it could not exist if I got anything back. It would make it less pure. Her beauty is burning so bright lately, I feel utterly alienated. It frightens me.

And add to that the way I feel about Drew. I feel like I have a permanent albatross fastened around my neck. The albatross is fashioned from the most delicate Tiffany silver. That's how they tricked me. That's how they got me to put it on in the first place. The bird is slim and neat and sparkles on my throat. Even if I could get rid of it, I wouldn't want to. It looks pretty fabulous, besides.

Drew's osmosis into my life beats even Treena's. It's like Treena has been shrunk and compacted and made more intensely obsessable. Drew and Treena. It's just too much to think about. They both crept through my ears and into my brain. And they're not happy about sharing the space. I can feel them kicking and fighting and tossing sarcastic asides across my cranium. It's like having different-coloured bright lights flashed off and on. I feel dizzy and nauseous all the time. Both of them are there and I need them, but I don't want to see them. They are so powerful that they don't make things clearer, they make things murkier. I can't see where I am. They are blinding me.

I try to turn down the light myself, use willpower, like I used to will myself to change the channel when I was having a nightmare. But now it's nightmares during the day, about the gingerbread house with posters of Marilyn Monroe and Elizabeth Taylor, sliding to the floor because the walls are too sweet to hold the Blu-Tack. Instead of trying not to step on pavement cracks, I am trying not to step on Liz Taylor's face. Her photos are sliding and I'm trying to avoid them, but when I look down, I'm standing on her eyes.

NINE

I went round to Ray's because I thought he might have some idea what Drew was up to. But within minutes we were rowing about Tommy again even though he was only next door buying cigarettes. He never had a go at Tommy for being so rude to me in Edinburgh. "Look, I told you, I don't want to talk about it. He's a good boy. He's been there for me."

Ever since Ray made it, he's been there. Before then, when they were first starting out, Tommy gave Ray a terrible review:

> Ray is retro without any romance or respect for the bands he is ripping off (Beatles/Beatles/Beatles). Ray could just about get away with "Yeah, yeah, yeah!" But he hasn't the energy, intelligence, or depth to carry off the White Album. Who wants to hear fourth-rate psychedelia, anyway? Incidentally, Mr. Devlin is exactly what you'd expect of a Cambridge graduate—he is a pretentious, graceless slob. Mundane by name. Mundane by nature.

He didn't even bother to slag him off properly, such was his lack of interest. Ray smashed up a whole pub when he read it, which the record company paid for, and offered a bounty on Tommy's head, which they didn't pay for.

Despite the review, Ray began to take off and within the year had had two Top 10 hits and been on *Top of the Pops* three times. Tommy began to come round to him. "Yeah, he's coming on, man. Obviously been listening to some Faces. Must have run out of other cats to rip off." Then Tommy found out he was from the same village as Ray and Ray found out they supported the same team and they became best mates and now Ray only gets brilliant reviews. They have both wiped that first review from their minds.

When I got to the house, Tommy was apologising for the review Ray got in Edinburgh and the unfavourable comparisons with Drew, even though he didn't write it and hadn't even seen it before it went to press. Ray slumped in the couch, his head in his hands, as Tommy bounced around him, a ludicrous purple scarf tucked into his suit, spitting and gesticulating wildly.

"That jerk, slagging you off, just trying to make a name for himself. He's just championing this little art-house kid. Ray, man, people are always going to have trouble with a singer who has guts, who has soul. Look at how they treated Dexys, man, and The Happy Mondays. Look at the shit they gave The Clash towards the end."

"The end?" wailed Ray. Ray's anxiety hit Tommy in the gut, as if he were a mother watching her only child being rejected in the school playground. He tried again.

"All the way through. You know what I'm saying. Build 'em up, knock 'em down. But that's what the *NME* is there for.

What do they know? It ain't what it used to be. Who buys it apart from students, anyway? It doesn't mean anything. But don't worry. I gave the little bastard a dressing down. I won't give him any feature work."

Tommy didn't explain why, if the NME was so insignificant, he had been there for over two decades. Neither did he mention that the reason he wouldn't give the bastard any feature work was because, despite his two decades' service, he was still not in a position to do so. Ray, however, seemed soothed by Tommy's dulcet, mod tones, and gave up rubbing his temples, stood up, and began to slap Tommy vigorously on the back, as if to stop him choking on bread.

"Thanks, Tommy, man. I just thought it was really unfair. He wasn't listening to the message." Ray is such a jerk when he hangs around with Tommy. "What message? What message wasn't he listening to?" I asked. "Your answerphone message? I'm not surprised. It goes on for so long. The message in a bottle?"

I did my best impression of Sting, kneeling on the floor with my arms over my knees in one of the three yoga positions I know. Ray burst out laughing and started hopping about the room, squealing, "Ey oh-oh, ey oh-oh, ey oh-oh."

"String! String! I am String!" we coughed, fluffing up our hair in the mirror.

Ray and I find Sting endlessly amusing. We are also reduced to girl giggles by MTV presenters, endive salad, and Puff Daddy being a rapper even though he has buck teeth. Tommy watched nervously. He couldn't join in because it would crumple his suit. It was clear he didn't want to in any case. I could see his little mind racing: "They look like fools. Yet Ray is clearly enjoying himself. I should join in. But I can't. They look like fools."

Tommy watched me hopping and started his bristling. Then the phone rang and that's how Tommy Belucci came to be there when Ray told me what had happened to Drew. Tommy Belucci is always there, especially when I don't want him to be. I stared at him as Ray answered the cordless phone in the kitchen. He couldn't look at me. If I'd been wearing a low-cut dress, at least he would have somewhere to look. But I was wearing my school uniform. Not in an ironic, saucy way, but in a "I have just got back from an afternoon of double French, therefore I am wearing my school uniform" way.

Funny. The blazer, skirt, and tie become automatically sexy the minute you leave school, when you're eighteen or nineteen and pull it out for fancy-dress parties. But whilst you're still there, stewing through Maths, unable to find any-one who'll let you sit next to them in the cafeteria, crying in the toilet stalls, you know what it represents and you can't bring yourself to make it look alluring. That would be traitor-ous and phoney. I knew I looked like shit and I was glad I did because that's how the twenty pounds of grey polyester and itchy navy wool made me feel.

Tommy watched the TV screen. He never talks to me. At first, he simply did not know how to address me. He still doesn't know, but he has decided he doesn't like me. I hated him from the first second I spent in his company. Some people are born with natural charisma. This boy has negative charisma. He walks into a room and the oxygen starts to evaporate. I guess that's why girls sleep with him. They find his awfulness quite transfixing. He's like a lousy 1970s disaster movie that they can't bring themselves to turn off, even though it is making their life worse every minute they leave it on.

Tommy can't figure out why I am there, what purpose I serve. I know what he's thinking: *If Ray wants to shag teenage girls, that's fine, par for the course and all, so long as he lets his mates have some too.* Personally, if I were a grown man, I would not care to make love to teenage girls. I absolutely can't see how it makes them feel younger, unless, as I imagine it, it makes them feel very, very stupid and that, in itself, takes them back to adolescence. Of course, I understand perfectly why a young girl should sleep with an older man.

Teenage boys are never grateful—for your presence, for your beauty, for your thoughts, for your breath. They aren't even thankful if you give in and do the deed, not just afterwards, but during. Which doesn't make sense. Surely the younger you are, the less chance you've had to have sex, the more excited you should be about it. Teenage boys should be prostrate at our feet, trembling with feverish anticipation. Yet when they do coerce their classmates into bed, they seem terribly underwhelmed about it. At best, teenage sex is an achievement on a par with scoring a goal at a Saturday football match. The goal posts consist of two empty Coke cans. The referee is a three-legged dog. At worst, teenage boys see sex as a duty, no more inspiring than taking out the rubbish.

Men, on the other hand, give that one little act unbelievable significance. You can spot the man having an affair with a young girl because he is the one struck dumb (and I do mean dumb) with inspiration—they get inspired to paint, to cut their hair, to change their job, to write a song or a poem or a novel that never gets published. If a sixteen-year-old girl tells a forty-year-old man to read this or that book, because it's her favourite, he will read it, whether it's *Wuthering Heights* or *Valley of the Dolls*. When you're forty, you suddenly feel very strongly that young people should be taken seriously.

If you are going to have an affair with an older man, make sure you do it before you yourself get too old. I always think it's the girl who really risks looking silly in those relationships. When I see a twenty-two-year-old girl dining with a middle-aged man, I think, "Jesus, girl, you're too old to be doing that. He's just a goofy guy, but you should know better." Lolita was twelve when she began her affair with Humbert. She died in childbirth at the age of seventeen. Abigail Williams was eleven when her sixty-five-year-old lover, John Proctor, spurned her, messing with her eleven-year-old mind and causing her to spark the Salem witch hunts. What I'm saying is, if you want to play Lolita, you can't be older than sixteen, and even that's pushing it. If you have to toy with such a cliché, you might as well get it right. Do it properly. The key thing to remember is, you never actually have to have sex. Indeed, if you are playing the game correctly, it shouldn't even cross your mind. As any Lolita knows, it's all about tormenting the man, not the other way around.

I used to love older men when I was ten or eleven. I would flirt outrageously with the builders who were redoing the kitchen in our house in London. It was the middle of a particularly sweltering summer, and I'd make regular trips to the refrigerator, whilst wearing my knickers and vest and heart-shaped glasses. "Oh, hi, boys!" I'd coo on my way out. I don't know who the hapless construction workers were more frightened of, me or Manny. I also enjoyed a long-running romance with my Physical Education teacher.

He was truly gorgeous, with a broken nose and spinach-green eyes. People said he was "rugged," which, in my mind, had as much to do with his love of rugby as his jutting jaw. All the mothers made a big fuss over him, wearing five-inch heels and splashing themselves in Chanel when they came to pick their kids up from extra gym. He never looked them in the eye or responded to their come-ons, and got away as soon as was possibly polite. He was, I knew all along, madly in love with me.

I knew he loved me, because no matter how many times he cornered me in the gym changing-room or on a cross-country run, he would never make me touch him there, in that most pathetic and lonely of places. He was a poet, not a pervert. Instead, he'd make me touch his ears, to prove how much they burned when I was near him. For my part, I did little to discourage him. I would suck on lollipops and leave my laces untied so he would have to kneel at my feet and tie them, and I'd turn up for class with a Hello Kitty plaster on my knee.

It was never taken to any kind of conclusion. I did think he was handsome, but I was mostly interested in tormenting him. The day I left and headed off for secondary school, he couldn't even look at me. I *was* a sexy kid. I found a photograph of me and him at the school sports day. He is grabbing me, swinging me in the air, with his arms wrapped around my thighs, holding me close. His arms are flexed and bulging with muscles. His white V-necked T-shirt is wet against his taut chest because I had been squirting him with a water pistol. Thank God I knew when to stop. Aged twelve. Sometimes

I have horrible visions of Treena, dressed coquettishly and acting all kittenish, aged fifty-two.

I would do it, I would sleep with old men, if it meant I were admired. Which is all I want in life, for Lord's sake. I'd like to be told I'm gorgeous and stunningly clever and quite, quite different from any other woman on earth. Or that I have nice-smelling hair. Ray admires me when he's in a good mood, but I would never take advantage of him. I'm not stupid. I know he'd admire me less, or not at all, if anything sexual ever happened. But it's silly even talking about it. Not only is Tommy barred from talking to me, Ray isn't even shagging me either. So he gets no piece of that action. Tommy can't work out the deal and that bothers him. He presumed I was besotted with Ray, and Ray, being too kind for his own good, was humouring me.

Of course, there was always the possibility that Ray and I might really and sincerely like each other, that there might be things Ray talked about to me that he felt he couldn't discuss with Tommy. It haunted Tommy late at night, when he sensed the ghost of his father under his bed and when the traffic lights changed too soon and he thought he was about to die in a car crash, that there were things Ray didn't share with him.

He had to know the release date of the album, which venues had been pencilled in for the tour dates, and which song had been chosen as the first single, or he felt violently ill, as if a lump of kryptonite had been slung around his neck. All his powers were gone and he could no longer defend himself—against work, against other writers, against women. His worst nightmare was that he would wake up one morning to find Ray had given an exclusive to another paper. But Tommy banished the thought from his mind. He eradicated from his mental files of grievances the possibility that Ray might like me better than he liked him. Blokes and chicks don't feel that way about each other. He reached across me for his cigarette packet.

"Oh, better that you don't, Tommy. Ray's got a sore throat at the moment. He can't afford to lose his voice. He's doing *Top of the Pops* tomorrow."

Tommy glared at me, but tucked his cigarettes into his inside coat pocket, no doubt so he could pull them out again in slow motion later that night. He grabbed the remote control and turned the volume up on the television. Boys always have to be in command of any implement of power. That's all they have, because women, as Manny told me, *are* the power. I stared at the back of his head, which is pointy and thoroughly unflattered by such a short haircut.

"Why, Tommy, have you had your hair snipped again?"

"Yeah," he mumbled, noncommittally, in case Ray noticed and decided he didn't like it.

"Again? Really?" Obviously he had. I could see and I had no reason to doubt his word, because whether or not you had your hair cut would be a stupid thing to lie about, even from Captain Stupid. So, as my French teacher is wont to tell me, I was being facetious.

"Yes. I cut it." He nervously touched his inch-long locks. "Why?"

"Oh, nothing. It just looks so lovely and curly."

Tommy's face dropped. He gasped for breath.

"Tommy, I thought you mods didn't go for curls. But it looks lovely. Very romantic. Very Marc Bolan." He was about to storm out of the room when Ray came back in, sucking on his lip.

"Everything all right, man?"

Ray shuffled from foot to foot, looking past Tommy to me. Like a magnet, Tommy followed his gaze.

"What's happened?" I blurted.

"Oh, shit," said Ray.

"What? Was that Manny? What have I done?"

Ray scratched his forehead with his thumb. "It's not you. Seems our boy has got himself in trouble."

I heard my breath, too fast and stumbly. "Which boy?"

Ray's breathing became slower and more deliberate, as if we were a little front-room ecosystem. Tommy had no place in it, but he wouldn't leave. "Your friend. Drew. Look, Viva, I didn't want to tell you. But remember that Kindness of Strangers gig in King's Cross?"

"Yes."

"Well, I didn't see him after that."

"So?"

"Well, neither did anyone else."

There was a dot of blood in the middle of Ray's head where his nail had been digging.

"What?" I screeched, the kind of "What?" that Joan Crawford gave before she beat her children with wire hangers. My eyes blazed and Ray began to back out of the room.

"He's been missing for a week or so now. We all figured, he's a grownup. He can take care of himself."

"Yeah." I felt myself start to hyperventilate.

"But that was my manager. Apparently they just found his clothes on the end of Brighton Pier. They're assuming . . ."

I couldn't breathe. I wanted to say "Paper bag" but it came out "Beer," which I don't even drink. Ray went gladly to the kitchen. I followed him with shoes full of wet cement and a heart full of glass. I leaned against the kitchen door. Ray pulled a beer out of the fridge and handed it to me. I dropped it on the floor and watched as the green glass smashed and the foul beige liquid spread silently towards the stove, not wanting to get involved. We both watched it.

Tommy crept in and stood by the push bin, wanting to offer Ray support and also to be sure not to miss anything, all the while trying to look surreptitious. I spun around. "Yes, Tommy, I have noticed you standing there in your fucking funeral suit, you mod fucking cunt bastard."

He put his arm across Ray, as if he were the one this was happening to. Through the layer of ice forming fast across my body like a shield, I stared at him, bore two holes into his face, one deep into each eye. I bored and bored and wrote on his forehead in blistering hate, "Leave this house now or I will kill you dead," but he stayed rooted to the lino.

I turned my back on both of them and held cold metal hands with the fridge door.

I gasped, "What do you think has happened?"

"I don't know," Ray whispered, as if whispers made it only half true.

"What?"

"I don't know." I was the casting director and Ray was the nervous drama-school graduate, speaking too softly and then too loud, booming on the wrong words, like a parody of Laurence Olivier. A kid doing Olivier badly.

I started to sway. "He could just have left the country, couldn't he?"

"Maybe. He made good money on this tour, I made certain of that. I made sure he wasn't ripped off. But now they've found his clothes in Brighton. That's where he lived."

"He lived in Brighton? He never told me that."

"Well, Viva, he didn't tell you everything because you didn't really know each other that well, did you? I know he looked after you in Edinburgh, but . . . Look. He had been drinking in the bar of a hotel in Brighton. He went out to the pier and no one ever saw him again. That's all I know."

I interrupted him, sobbing, "Oh my God."

Through my splutters I heard Tommy's malevolent voice. "You were right not to tell her before, chief. If the kid's this upset, she'd only have worked herself into a total state."

"Leave it alone, Tommy," Ray hissed. If I had been paying attention, if I hadn't been so distraught, that hiss would have pleased me no end. But all I heard was that Ray knew all along. Tommy, for fuck's sake, knew all along. This event that I had been so busy foreseeing had actually happened, and nobody had bothered to let me know.

I turned and pointed at Tommy, like a sniffer dog who, instead of heroin, had been trained to pick up the scent of evil mods. "And he knew and I didn't."

"I had to know," Tommy huffed. "I'm from the *NME*. It's news."

Ray glanced up.

Tommy caught himself. "But not that big news."

Ray sighed, a big man's sigh, bigger and louder than a young girl's tears. "Viva, I don't understand why you're making such a big deal of this. You met the guy twice."

"Yeah, but he changed my life."

"Come off it, Viva. He told you about French situationism and he tried to shag you."

That was too much. I ran out of the kitchen, down the stairs, and onto the street, my expensive scarf uncoiling from my neck and dropping to the pavement, my snot flying behind me like an expensive scarf. I had one exam left and no one to love. God, if I had just shagged him, that would be easy. At least he would have left me something, something I could put a name to. But it's true, all we had was one night. If I was pregnant, if I had his baby, then I would have a legitimate reason to be destroyed. Everyone would feel sorry for me and I would have part of him forever.

But all we had was talk. Just words, from two people who wanted to be able to write it down but hadn't the dedication or the courage. If all you are is lazy, then there's always the possibility that you might one day overcome it and do something great with your life. Even when you're ninety, and lying in bed watching reruns of $M*A*S*H$, you can still say, "Hey, today is the day I get up and write my masterpiece." But if you lack courage, that's it, that's final, it's out of your hands. It isn't going to come to you in the night and there's no way you can make it without it. Soul-destroying for someone like Drew. All those thoughts, for what? For who? For himself, at 1:30 A.M. in front of the BBC1 close-down?

I was honoured that he shared his thoughts with me, even

though I could see how it was for him—that it wasn't a case of sharing, but of giving them away: "Closing-Down Sale: Everything Must Go." Ray's right, I could have been anyone. But not anyone would have been interested, and I congratulated myself for wanting to hear. And then I couldn't stop listening. As the alcohol thickened his tongue, I had all but begged him to stay awake, to keep talking. I already knew it was a lost cause, that I was witness to a dying man's last words.

So I tried to write down as much of our talk as I could remember, but I know I missed a lot of it. Words are slippery and disloyal. As soon as they came out of his mouth, they made a run for the door, and finding it closed, slipped under the crack for the light. Everyone wants to be in the light, apart from potatoes and moles. And Drew. Who was too weak to fight, and embraced the darkness, the failure, and the nightmares, and let the soil consume him and fall into his mouth.

In the back of his head he always thought, "The soil will take me and then I will finally be able to make my mark. If I have roots, I can bloom. I shouldn't fight it."

My misery carried me home, told me when to change lines on the underground and when to get off and how to slot my ticket into the machine. Treena says that when she is at her most drunk, she manages to do the most surprising things. The next day she can't work out how she made it home in one piece, or how she managed to paint such an excellent picture, or pick out such a pretty outfit at Miss Selfridge, or find the money to pay for it. I put my key in the door. "Why didn't I sleep with him? Why didn't I sleep with him?"

Manny looked excitedly up from his paper. "Why didn't you sleep with who?"

Ten

I should have slept with him because now he's dead and I will never lose my virginity and I will never, ever have a Drew-faced kid, which is the only thing that could have kept me sane. Like Priscilla Beaulieu—she's got a Presley-faced kid. Lisa Marie is undeniable proof that her mother did enjoy a long and passionate relationship with the King. Her black hair and Roman nose and weight battle are there in sharp focus in case Priscilla is one day loading the dishwasher and it suddenly strikes her that she might have made the whole thing up. That really she's just a housewife in Iowa who saw the newsreel of Elvis joining the army, and invented this story inside her head. If she ever thinks that, then she only has to see her baby to know she hasn't misremembered her whole life.

And America had JFK Jr., standing there, looking exactly like the best parts of both his parents. So if the country ever woke up fearful that they had dreamed Camelot, that John and Jackie were an invention, as intoxicating as the war against Communism and as comforting as Ronald McDonald, they only had to get the *National Enquirer* to stand outside his TriBeCa loft and get another shot of John-John putting out the trash. I don't know what they're going to do now. Why is it that the most photographed and celebrated and media-documented couples always produce children who look exactly like them? In terms of ensuring a permanent place in the history books, they're the ones least in need of carbon-copy kids. It's just God being flashy. Manny says I don't look anything like my mum.

If only I had a tiny, dark, and surly Drew-faced kid to keep under my pillow. I wouldn't feel so lonely. It's not the sex I'm interested in, it's the genes. Okay, I am interested in the sex, so far as it's some proof that I knew him. Like when someone says, "Have you read *War and Peace?*" or "Have you seen *Jules et Jim?*," you either have or you haven't. No one's the least bit impressed if your answer is "Well, it's on my bookshelf and I pick it up and look at it sometimes" or "I've seen the poster." If you've slept with someone, you have something definite, something containable. If you haven't, well, it's your word against the world. "I only spent one night with him, and we didn't even kiss, but we talked until he passed out." You can hardly expect the nation to gasp, "Now we see why you're so upset." I should have slept with him. There is no point in falling over and cutting your knee if you haven't got a scar to show for it.

But, my God, he would have been bad in bed. Rather, he would have been sad in bed, disgusted at the act and bewildered by how he got to it and desperate to know if he could get out of it. That night in Edinburgh, as his eyes rolled in their sockets, I asked him what he remembered of losing his virginity. He looked like he was going to be sick, then at the last moment he caught himself and smiled. "All I remember is that she made me a lovely bacon sandwich afterwards."

Killing yourself is a pretty good way to get out of having to see someone after you've had sex with them. I shall have to become a high-class prostitute. If I'm not that bothered about sex anyway, why not make some money out of it? Being a slut is the best insurance against being gossiped about. If you sleep with everyone, then no one cares. No one is interested. But if you never sleep with anyone, when you finally do, it's all over town. And then you're a slut.

Men will pay me for sex and I will close my eyes and clench my fists and curl my toes, like I am having a tooth pulled. Treena says men prefer it that way anyway. She says if she ever gets too into it, they look at her funny. "Calm down," said one, nervously, as she flung herself around the room.

Better to be paid. Why not be a kept woman? I treat myself like I'm my own mistress anyway. If Drew related to Blanche DuBois so much, I can do that, as they say in *Chorus Line*. Since he went missing, I spend all my money on gold-plated hair-grips and perfume and shoes that I only ever wear to watch TV. And they do make me feel brilliant. When I come home from school, take my Doc Martens off and put on fake satin mules with the marabou trim, slip into my dressing gown and my movie, I feel serene. I hold a glass of Coke to my cheek and pretend it is a glass of bourbon and I am in New Orleans. My bedroom door is the doorway onto the street and at night I can't sleep because of the heat and the commotion in this town.

So I go down to the river and dance as a man with scars on his face plays an accordion. People clap along and wolf-whistle and I whip my skirt around my thighs, which are long and lean because I barely get a chance to eat, what with all my bourbon and afternoon baths. I dance until my mules get muddy, then I tiptoe home, followed by sailors and men who have won hundreds of thousands of dollars playing stud poker. Steve McQueen might be there. I can't remember. I get confused at this point. Too much drink. I'm sure Karl Malden is lurking in the background, gazing at me longingly. I am kind to him because his mother is dying.

Manny asks me to close my door if I'm planning on acting out Tennessee Williams all night. But I leave it open. That's the point. The door has to be ajar so that the town can see me, so the men can admire me and the women can gossip. Yes, I will be a kept woman and then I will be able to afford my designer black outfits. A new client may bring me a box of expensive chocolates or a bottle of scent, but the ones I've had for years know to bring with them ebony earrings or agate crucifixes or panties the colour of ink. A lover might sometimes tempt me to wear maroon or pale blue, but I will spin away from him. "How dare you insult Drew's memory? I may sleep with you, but there is only one man in my life and he doesn't like maroon. He watches us as you paw me and he laughs at you, because you are nothing compared to him. And as I grit my teeth from the weight of your foul body pressing into my lungs, he takes my hand and says, 'Viva, black is beautiful on you.'"

And for two days after Ray told me about Drew's suicide, that's what I thought would become of me. That was my future, my life, as I rocked back and forth against Manny's armpit. Oh well, at least I wouldn't have any decisions to make: about university, about jobs, about lovers. My career was in my bedroom, lighting candles for a dead man who didn't know me, who I hardly know, and who no one else had heard of either.

I cried in the morning, when I brushed my teeth, and couldn't help wondering what Drew thought about toothbrushes and teeth in general. I wept when I went to school, because Drew was an intellectual and I never would be. No matter how hard I tried to listen in French class, in tribute to Drew, all I could hear was a vague tinnitus ring reverberating around the class-room. I cried when I got home and fixed myself a peanut but-ter, jelly, and Fluffernutter marshmallow spread sandwich on white bread, because Drew was so thin and that was something else I would never be.

I cried when Manny tried to talk to me and when Manny tried to listen. Most especially I cried when I listened to the crappy vinyl Kindness of Strangers single Drew had given me that night in Edinburgh. It had a scratch straight down the middle. It sounded like Drew had hiccups. I laughed through my tears. Then I cried some more because I felt so guilty for having laughed. Drew did not, perhaps, have as many options open to him as I had at first imagined. He was smart, he must have had the world at his feet. But that's not how it works. He was smart, really, really smart. So he had nothing. His plans and his ideas and his theses and schemes backed him into a corner, held a flick-knife to his throat, and told him he had no choice but to leave town.

And then it struck me. If you're being forced out of town, if they're really going to get you if you stay, then you don't want to suffer the indignity of having them drive you to the state line. You want to find your own way out. You'll do what they want, but you'll do it your way. In that second I saw that suicide wasn't his way. If you believe that people are more honest when they are drunk, then you also believe that you can get more truth out of someone in the first three hours of meeting them than in thirty years of knowing them.

Suicide was Jean Seberg or Brian Jones or someone in a seventies glam rock band, but it just wasn't him. I knew that Drew would talk about suicide for as long as he had the power of speech, even if no one was listening. For as long as he was conscious. But he would not do it. Of that I was certain. We were more similar than I had thought, although that brought me curious little comfort. Again, I felt uncomfortable because I knew for sure I was stronger than him. Because I wasn't ashamed. I am not ashamed to be all talk and no action. He was.

Treena was completely unhelpful. Like Ray, she resents me being interested in anyone but her. And she hates hysterics. So long as they're drug- or alcohol-fueled, they're okay. But real hysteria, from the pit of your stomach, turns her off so much that she can barely stand to speak to me.

Standing in the kitchen, I clutched a grease-stained fish dish in the half-full sink and listened attentively as my breath started to quicken. I was so caught up in the sound of my own breath that I didn't hear the dish smash. I do not suit doing the washing up. I have never particularly cared for kitchen-sink drama. It is no place for a girl like me. Manny, who was skimming over the paper, stood to attention, terrified that I was going to start crying again. I couldn't have even if I'd wanted to. Even if I'd imagined that I had a pet puppy and it had been run over and then bitten by a rat, I couldn't have wept another tear. All the tears were gone, as if sucked out by a tiny dental vacuum. Who needs professional medics? How clever the human body is by itself. The absence of tears was a medical precaution. I couldn't cry or I wouldn't be able to think properly. Manny gripped my arm, but my arm was stronger than his grip and he let go.

"Viva, please, I'm trying to understand. But you're making yourself hysterical. You're making yourself ill with your *schreying*. Your body can't take anymore. The skin around your nose is peeling off and you've burst a blood vessel in your cheek. So please, try to stop. Try to stay calm. Or at least let me be excused. You come and knock on my door when you're finished and we'll have a cuddle. I don't want you to be unhappy. But I'm obviously not helping. And I can't watch you do it again."

"I'm not going to cry," I sniffed. "There's nothing to cry about."

"Viva, there had better have been something to cry about. Tears aren't like Marks & Spencer's nighties. You can't get your money back if they don't fit you."

"Listen, okay. Wait. I . . . I shouldn't have got myself so distraught. It isn't as bad as I thought."

"Good girl. Smart girl. There are lots of tortured, unsuccessful artists in the world to choose from."

"No, that's not what I mean, although I take your point. Okay, Manny. The thing is, I don't think he is dead."

Manny took my hand in his. "No, baby. He is. He's dead. He jumped off Brighton Pier. Although I'm sure he'll always be alive in your heart."

I gripped his hand tight, digging my little fingernail in not so much that he'd know I was doing it deliberately but enough so he would wake up and listen. My melancholy had wrapped us both up and cosied us down like the quilt Manny throws over us when we watch *Seinfeld* on cable.

"No, he's not dead. He didn't kill himself. He wanted us to think he did so we wouldn't try and find him. He's alive." I drew a breath but didn't look up.

"But, the thing is, he won't always be alive in my heart, not unless I can find him. I haven't got enough heart anymore. I haven't got enough of him to keep alive. He never gave me anything. I asked if I could borrow one of his books, but he wouldn't let me, said he was still reading them. All of them. Even if I had stolen just an eye pencil, I'd have enough to last me another year."

Manny pulled me to him, gripped his arms around my shoulders, and started talking quietly into my hair. "Viva, listen to me." I wasn't listening because his grip was alarming to me. It was a very heterosexual, Jack Nicholson thing to do — bear-hugging me and breathing into my ear at the same time. "People were always obsessed with me, not the other way around. Are you sure that's what you want to be? Once you start on that track, it's very hard to get off. And as much fun as it looks to be the obsessor, it takes more guts to be adored, trust me."

"I do trust you, but I know what I feel. I know my destiny. This task has my name on it."

"No, it has someone else's name on it. It always will. You're setting yourself up for a lot of tasks." He looked very sad. I felt, for probably the first time in my life, that I had let him down. In the past he'd said I had let him down: when I left all the dishes in the sink for a week when he was in Florida, or when I decided to cut my own hair, based on a photo of Louise Brooks, and ended up looking like Prince Valiant. That's not really a letdown—adults expect that of you.

There have been little failures on a daily basis. Broken soup bowls, congealed yoghurt, turned orange juice, jelly in the peanut butter, shoes pulled off without untying the laces, overflowing laundry bin, expensive sunglasses with one lens crushed, chocolate for breakfast. And not just chocolate— bad, cheap, nasty "chocolate-flavoured" corner-store confectionery.

Most often, there are aesthetic differences of opinion. For instance, an adult's perception of a room as looking like a pigsty, versus a child's belief that a mess is the best place to hide happiness you want to come back to later. Use the pile of dirty knickers and odd socks to conceal the ring Treena swapped with you, the necklace Manny gave you for your fourteenth, the report card where Mr. Edwards says you have a natural flair for Chartism. You thought they were gone for good? Think how delighted you'll be when you see them again. Childhood is tiring. You have very little actual power. You need the controlled chaos of your bedroom to keep you going.

Manny headed upstairs for bed. He looked old. I got the heart-pounding fear I used to have when I was eight, that one day he will die. How selfish of him. How can I put all my trust in someone who would do something so selfish as die?

"Viva, this is not within my realm of experience. I don't know how I can help you. If you really believe that Drew is still with us, you believe it. Who's to say? It would be nice if you were right. Oh, Viva. Sometimes I feel so sad for you, being raised by me, not having a woman in the house."

I don't think he felt sad, I think he just didn't know what to say. He was clutching at any word that might bring me back. He was going to say all of them, including "haystack" and "banana split," in the vain hope that one of them would be the word that worked. I did that in my Biology exam last year. I didn't know anything and I hadn't done any work, so I put "nitrogen oxide" as the answer to every question because, since there were 103 questions, statistically, I was bound to be right eventually. So Manny had pulled the "needing a mother figure" card.

"We have her." I pointed at Liz, whose photo was framed on our living-room wall. "And," I shrugged my shoulders cheerfully, "I have Ray."

Manny didn't even turn around to laugh. "He's not a woman."

"No, but he has woman's hair."

He does. Over the last few months he has allowed it to grow to his shoulders. A lot of men have shoulder-length hair. But for some reason, Ray has had his shaped, at a very expensive salon. It sways and shines like a Pantene model's. It is weird. It makes you want to touch the hair and forget about the man. It makes you feel unclean, which is not how a woman likes to feel in the presence of a man. One doesn't like to think that an attractive man has done anything to make himself so—he should just wake up that way. When you see Ray's hair, you see him in the shower, lathered up, rinsed out, in front of the mirror, with gel and a blow-drier. Insanity, drunkenness, and preening are three attributes that are quite attractive on women but thoroughly disagreeable on men.

Ray came over at seven for dinner and he brought his woman's hair with him. It is very healthy, and highlighted the glaring truth that the rest of him looks less so. He too looked old. Crow's feet dug into the corners of his eyes and there were drooping lines of flesh on either side of his mouth. Weird to think they came from smiling. I was suddenly very embarrassed at how young I look. Which is stupid, because I'm a teenage girl. What were they expecting? Joan Rivers? I think they were. I realise how much my youth hurts them: Ray, Tommy, Drew, even Manny. Not Treena. She doesn't see faces, not her own in the mirror or anyone else's, just blurs of colour and form, shadow and light. "She looks like Winona Ryder," she told a boy, grabbing my arm, as if she were trying to sell me. "He looks like Will Smith," she told me, pointing at the boy. He didn't and I don't but it struck me that she really thought it. I asked her why she thought I looked like Winona Ryder and she said, "I dunno. You're little. And you've got dark hair."

I looked at Ray, his face haggard and body language sheep-ish. I felt sorry for him having to be friends with me, having me as a responsibility. Tommy was right to be suspicious. Ray wasn't getting anything out of this, out of me. "Ray . . ."

He looked so worried. I decided to spit it out.

"Ray, I don't mean to go all Shirley MacLaine on you, but tonight, when I was doing the dishes, I had a major insight. I know that Drew isn't dead. He didn't kill himself. I know it."

Ray blinked and put his hand up to shield his face from the

kitchen light and the craziness coming off me. "What do you know?"

"I know. Like I know the correct order of Elizabeth Taylor's husbands. It's just something inside me that I could never un-know."

"Viva, they found his clothes on the end of Brighton Pier." He stretched each syllable and held my gaze, to check that I was following. He must have spent the evening with Tommy.

"Okay, but did they find his body?"

"No, but it could have been carried out to sea. The currents are strong." He was quiet and calm. He was almost smiling again.

"Ray, I promise you, I know I'm right. I would have more proof if you had told me sooner. But you can make it up to me. I need a favour. Will you take me to Brighton for the weekend?"

"What?" he spluttered.

I pulled my bra strap up from the edge of my shoulder, catching it with my thumb before it went into free fall. "I want to go to Brighton. I need to see where it was that Drew's switch was flicked. I need to be where he decided to do it. You have to come with me. You have a responsibility."

ELEVEN

We drove to Brighton. I felt sick all the way. Ray's car is full of empty cheese and onion crisp packets and his radio is jammed to Capital FM, which fades to a hiss once you get past Burgh Heath. I put my feet on the dashboard and he snapped at me to sit up properly or he would take me home.

I went very quiet for half an hour. Then I pulled my eyebrows down over my eyes and whimpered, "I want to see the hotel where he was drinking," with the same voice and expression I used at age four to demand ice cream.

He should have told me off, but instead he chose to ignore me. He doesn't even find me cute anymore. When I first met Ray, he thought I was adorable, just about the cutest thing he ever did see.

"Fucking hell, Viva. I could be back in London, at a party or having a shag. I've met a girl."

"Congratulations. I've met a girl before in my life too." I stared at his ear, behind which he had tucked his shiny hair and a half-smoked cigarette.

Then *he* shut up for half an hour until we were in Brighton, when he suddenly banged his hand against the wheel and exclaimed, "God. You bring so much baggage with you."

"I haven't brought anything," I smirked.

"I mean, emotional."

"I know what you mean."

"I know you know."

He was being so boring. "Oh God, shut up, Harold Pinter. Enough with the pregnant pauses. Fine. I don't see why this whole thing should be such hard work. If you're really my friend, you must want to help me find out what happened to the love of my life."

"The love of your life?" he screeched.

"Yes. I know you think I'm being a teenage girl. Well, you're right. That's exactly what I'm being. Okay, it's out of character and you find it a bit unsettling, but I think it's my right. People who work in offices are allowed five weeks' holiday a year. Five weeks a year I should be allowed to behave like a teenage girl and not like Norman Mailer, or whoever it is you keep confusing me with. You picked the wrong self-obsessed Jew."

He kept one arm on the steering wheel and looked slyly over at me, probably to check whether I was Viva and not Norman Mailer. "Fine, you've decided you're in love. Whatever. But this is serious. A man has taken his own life. Viva, it's not a picnic. You're talking like a cross between Ruth Rendell and Enid Blyton. You want murder and chips."

"I don't bloody want murder. That's the last thing I want. I hadn't even thought of it. Damn, now I have to wonder about that too. Thanks a lot, Ray. By the way, I do want chips."

We parked in Ship Street and found a good chip shop, which is not hard to do in Brighton, and sat on the pebbles with our two-pronged forks.

"Pebbles. How stupid," Ray muttered through a mouth full of potato squish.

"Ray. How eloquent."

He threw down his fork. The pathetic wooden stick didn't even make a sound as it hit the beach. No one ever notices when Ray throws down a gauntlet. It's not that he doesn't throw hard enough. It's just that he always picks such tiny gauntlets to throw. "Look, I don't have to be here. I'm doing you a bloody favour."

"Okay, okay." I tossed a fat pebble into the slate grey sea, which splished on and on, for no good reason, like a Tom Hanks film. I popped another chip in my mouth. The vinegar stung the back of my throat and made my eyes water, like one of Treena's Prodigy records played at full volume. "So who's the girl?"

"Oh, just some girl I've had my eye on for a while. She's beautiful. So beautiful you feel very lonely when you look at her." He picked at his sneaker, pulling the A out of the rubberized Adidas logo. "I've met her a couple of times, but we've never really talked properly before. We bumped into each other at the Met Bar the other night and got chatting."

"The Met Bar? You went there of your own accord? God, you're so sad. Who chats at the Met Bar? Were you in the toilet?" I laughed so loud that some old people in deck chairs turned round and scowled.

"Yes. We were taking cocaine in the toilets. And then we had sex in the toilets."

"Oh my God, I don't want to know. You're disgusting. Sex in the toilets at the Met Bar? That's the worst thing I've ever heard."

"Worse than the war in Bosnia?"

"Yes."

"You're just jealous because you've never been to the Met Bar. You can't get in. You don't look old enough." Sometimes Ray really sounds exactly like the girls at school.

He said I looked too young, but that's not an insult. I knew what he really meant was that I wasn't pretty enough to get in. Tears sprung in my eyes, like Russian ballet stars. What a stupid thing for Ray to say. Surely it should be ugly girls who have sex in toilets. Because in the toilet everything is so ugly that they're bound to look better.

Ray looked embarrassed. Because he'd had sex in a toilet and because he knew he had made me feel bad and ugly. And if I felt ugly, I might eventually become ugly and then he would have to explain to everyone why he was hanging around with an ugly girl.

"Let's go on the dodgems!" he yelped and spit came out of his mouth. He pulled out his wallet to pay the man in the booth, and a wad of twenties fell out.

"Jesus," I hissed, "put it away."

Here we were on the pier where the love of my life disappeared, and Ray wanted to go on the dodgems.

I climbed gingerly into the car, which was about as well-kept as Ray's real car. With each bump, I leaned away from him. I was not enjoying myself. He kept looking over at me, the way I do with Treena when I take her to the movies. She never laughs when she's supposed to. "That's not funny," she says, and I feel very guilty and low, because it must be being in my presence that has made it not funny, since everyone else in the theatre is doubling up. Our dodgem was whacked so hard from behind that Ray bit his tongue. I refused to crack a smile. Ray finally gave up and drove slowly to the side of the circuit before our time was even up. We stepped out of the car wordlessly.

As I dusted myself down, I realised that there were kids everywhere, specifically teenage boys. My mortal enemies. They weren't there before. It was as if they had descended on the city en masse, from the sky, from a previously unreleased Alfred Hitchcock film, too terrifying for human eyes. If I had been feeling insecure all afternoon, I immediately felt incredibly self-conscious. The boys were probably laughing at my hair, at my shoes, at my body. They swigged from cans of beer and bottles of Thunderbird. They pushed each other and spat and wolf-whistled at every girl in sight. Even me. Although I know they were just being sarcastic. Even worse, several of them recognised Ray and pointed at us. They didn't say anything, just held their arms out in front of them, as if claiming their five pounds.

"Ray. What is going on? I thought this town was supposed to be full of old ladies. Why are there so many seventeen-year-old boys drunk at five in the afternoon? Is that a Brighton thing I didn't know about?"

"Skyline are playing tonight." He spat the words. He hates Dillon, the lead singer of Skyline, more than anyone in the world, more than Margaret Thatcher or Hitler or Jack Lemmon, because Dillon is more famous than he is, although he won't admit it—either that he's more famous or that he resents him for it. He just shakes his head and wails, "It's football-terrace music," as if he is a curator at the British Library watching Charlotte Brontë first editions being replaced by Jackie Collins.

He hates Skyline more than he loves Woody Allen. "I told you I really didn't want to be in Brighton this weekend. I know you don't like to mingle with the proles."

"You mean *you* don't like to mingle with Skyline!" I pulled up my hood and tied the cord tight so that the icy wind wouldn't cut my cheeks so badly and the teenage boys couldn't laugh at my face.

"Same thing. I hate that bloody Dillon. He's a cunt."

"Excuse me. Please don't use the female genitalia as a word of abuse."

"Viva, he's a cunt. And he looks like a geography teacher."

I thought of Mr. Edwards and how everyone at school thinks he looks like a rock star. "If he looks so much like a geography teacher, why was he on the cover of *Smash Hits* and *NME* in one week?"

"I don't know," raged Ray. "Those hack bastards probably all had crushes on their teachers."

"Ray, you're talking really weird. I don't like it. You always get het up about Dillon. What's the big deal? If you don't like him, you don't have to talk to him. Why do you hate him so much?"

"Because he's called Dillon. You can't be a pop star if you're called Dillon. Who's called Dillon? Who spells it that way?"

"Well, obviously he does. Why do you care?" I felt like a psychiatrist trying to get a twelve-year-old to explain why he kept yelling the word "fuck." Ray had no good justification, although he bit his nails and tried to think of one.

"He's always trying to get one up on me."

I stared at him. "Why would he try to get one up on you?

He *is* one up on you. You are quite famous, but they're massive. Skyline are bigger than anyone. They're probably the biggest band in Britain, apart from U2. Don't judge yourself by their standards. Anyway, Skyline are proles stuff. Even Treena likes them."

Ray shot me a daggers look, as if I were a bumpkin fool who could never understand the tormented soul of a poet, and then stormed up the road. The kids were still pointing. I had to run to catch up with him.

"What did I say?" I jogged alongside him because he wouldn't slow down or even look at me. I had to pull out all the stops. Ray would only react to intense flattery now. "You don't want to be as big as them, you always say that. It's football-terrace music. Sure, lads go out and get drunk and bellow out Skyline songs outside your window at one in the morning. Yeah, the tabloids love them and the *NME* loves them and everyone loves them. And the reason everyone loves them is because they make money for anyone who even breathes their name. You don't need that. You're not coarse enough to make music for the masses. But a lot of people do worship you. You're not that far behind. And the real difference is, you make music that teenage girls can dream to. That's much more important than lager-and-vindaloo anthems."

He stopped abruptly, which was good, because he was about to tread in dog shit, and reached over to hold my hand. "You're so sweet to me, Viva. You're the only one who's not out to fuck me over." His voice was quivering and he had tears in his eyes. Heads began to turn and so did my stomach.

"Don't worry, Ray. Nothing to get upset about."

A tear rolled down his face. He didn't try to catch it. "I'm sorry I've been grumpy. I know how much Drew meant to you. I'll take you to the hotel."

For the first three minutes in about three weeks, I actually had forgotten about Drew, and I felt good. I decided perhaps I ought to take a break from Drew obsession for the evening, so I could store up energy and really get into it bright and early the next day.

"Look, Ray, I've got a funny idea. Why don't we go and see Skyline play tonight?"

Ray shook his head and blinked away the last of the tears. "No way. Uh-uh. Me? Go and worship at the shrine of Skyline? Dillon would think it was hysterical. He'd tell all his Neanderthal mates. It would be in the gossip column of the *NME*."

"No, I don't think so. Look at it calmly. It would be the coolest thing you could do. It would show how little you care about them. Like, oh, you happened to be in Brighton, so you thought you'd stop by and see what all the fuss is about. Dillon would be impressed that you were there. He'd be really freaked out. You would have one over on him."

"Tommy would say I was consorting with the enemy."

"Oh, fuck Tommy. He does what you say, not the other way around, remember?"

Ray cocked his head and frowned.

"Stop frowning," I almost yelled, "those wrinkles aren't getting any better." But bearing in mind his fragile ego in the face of Dillon from Skyline, I thought better of it.

Ray frowned harder. "I thought we were here to find Drew."

"No, God no," I laughed, as if that were the most ridiculous thing in the world and it was Ray's idea, not mine, to come all the way to Brighton just to look at a hotel bar Drew had drunk in. "No, no. We're here to find Drew's aura." I thought that would make him giggle.

But he dropped my hand and barked, "Yeah, right, Viva." He made a horrible face, like the girls at school on non-uniform days as they scathingly eyed up my pencil skirt, kitten heels, and white mohair Elizabeth Taylor sweater. They always wore jeans and a little T-shirt with a slogan on it. What was the point of non-uniform day? They only wore a different uniform—they came as Lolita. Again and again, I'd rather go as Shelley Winters. "Right, Viva."

"It was an Andy Warhol reference, Ray. The aura? In *From A to B and Back Again.* Don't you remember?"

"No, I don't, and I don't care. Can we just not talk about celebrities for one minute? Jesus, Viva, you are the worst namedropper in the world. It's really hard to talk to you some-times."

I'm not, I thought. Ray is. Ray gets angry if I talk about someone more famous than him (Dillon) and he gets mad if I talk about someone less famous than him (Drew). I can't win. Sure, I drop names, but they're all dead people and B-movie actresses who haven't worked in thirty-seven years. Ray's the real namedropper. He's the one who goes to clubs and has sex in the toilets. He's the one who always goes to all the awards ceremonies even though "they're all bollocks." I've said to him, "So don't go. You have no obligation. Skyline never go," and he screams, "They can afford not to go. They can do anything they like. I have to go or the record company will start plotting against me and someone will spread rumours about me. I know it!" He accuses me of being celebrity-obsessed because it's the thing he most dislikes about himself. There's nothing I can say when he gets like that, so I just have to change the subject.

"I want some more chips."

We stood in line again and the girl frying the fish looked at us oddly.

"It's for her," he apologised.

"No," stammered the girl. "I was just wondering if I could have your autograph. I'm a big fan. I was too shy to ask when you came in before."

Ray grinned and pulled a Bic from the back pocket of his jeans. "Are you going to see Skyline tonight?"

"No way." The girl beamed. "I don't go for that hooligan music." Ray signed his autograph with a big heart and ten kisses. And suddenly, when the girl handed me my chips, he was prepared, even quite into the idea, of going to see Skyline.

Ray thought he knew the bloke who was roadying for Skyline—he'd done a European tour for him back when Ray was bigger than Dillon. He could get us in with the minimum of fuss. I tried to persuade Ray he should cause the maximum fuss, let the whole band know that he was really eager to watch them play, but he said, "You're such a drama queen. Let's do it my way."

We hovered outside the venue, looking for the stage door.

"I must know where it is. I've played here enough times."

We went round the back of the alleyway, where a gang of

thirty beer'd-up boys were chanting Skyline's last hit. "Flyyy higher than the staaars!" They jeered at us as we pushed past. I don't know who it was harder for—me or Ray.

The shaven-headed, thick-necked bulldog on the door laughed. "And what can I do for you? Want an autograph, do you?"

I could tell Ray was about to back down, so I fixed the bull-dog with my best PR-girl stare and ordered, "Just fetch Mole the roadie and tell him that Ray Devlin is here."

He nodded at Ray. "I know who you are. You can come in, so long as you promise not to start any fights." Ray nodded meekly. Yeah, right, Ray starts a fight. He couldn't win a match against a one-armed baby.

The corridor was dark and the walls were pasted with mouldy old tour posters, several of which had Ray's face on them. As we turned the corner, we could hear the sound of a guitar being tuned up and an extended drum solo, which the drummer was clearly enjoying, since it would never make it into the real show. We followed the music out to the front of the house.

And there was Dillon, at the back of the hall, clapping his hands. He didn't look like a geography teacher at all. In fact, he looked more like a substitute Religious Studies teacher, young and wiry and over-enthusiastic. His hair was dark blond and parted to the right. It was old man's hair on a very young face. He looked both older and younger than his twenty-eight years. His face was pleasant enough, but hardly there at all. Everything was so even: his eyes the same size as his nose, which was the same size as his mouth. If he were a criminal, he would never get caught, because he looked like anyone. It would be almost impossible to draw up an effective likeness. His frame was slight. He had tiny bird bones—skinny little arms and legs. His only outstanding feature was his skin, which was so pale, it almost glowed.

Dillon was the biggest star in pop, but there was something about him that suggested there had been a terrible mistake, and that the understudy had accidentally been allowed onstage without enough preparation. What on earth did the British record-buying public see in him? Why had all those boys chosen him to carry the burden of their dreams and ambitions on his slender shoulders? Then he saw us and snapped to life. A light went on in his grey eyes and he bounded over, bouncing, not like the waif that he was, but like a boxer. He pulled up two feet in front of Ray, and I saw that Dillon was a short-arse, barely reaching up to Ray's nose. Neither of them spoke. Then Dillon snapped his fingers in front of him and smiled.

"Y'all right, Raymond. Didn't think I'd see you here." He spoke with a Merseyside tinkle.

Ray shuffled backwards and forwards. "Well, we were in town. And my friend Viva's a fan." With utter disregard for any concept of subtlety, I stamped on his foot. I wasn't having that. I hadn't the slightest interest in Skyline, other than using them as a tool to help Ray conquer his fear of celebrity.

"Nice one," chirped Dillon, looking me over. I obviously didn't impress him, because he focused his attention back on Ray, just looking at him and grinning, a child who hadn't been taught it's rude to stare.

Then he reached out and shook Ray's hand, pulling him closer bit by bit. It looked like Ray had suffered a terrible industrial accident and had his arm caught in a machine. Dillon stopped at his elbow and pulled him into a hug. Ray was absolutely rigid.

"Top, Raymond, top. So I'll see you and your friend later. Come to the dressing room after the show. We'll have a beer. I've got a great new bird. She's a model. Been on the cover of Italian *Vogue* or summat. You've got to meet her. Boss tits. A right laugh."

Then he nodded at me and trundled off.

We scarpered out the front door, past the merchandising stall just being set up. We were both breathing as hard as two teenage girls who had just stolen a bagful of makeup from Woolies. As the Skyline fans pointed at us some more, which seemed all they were equipped to do, we started laughing so hard that I almost threw up. We dragged each other back into town.

Finally Ray managed to speak. "If Skyline are playing the same venues as me, they can't be that big."

I patted his back. Good old Ray. That was all he could think about. "Yeah, Ray, but you saw the advert in *NME*. You know what they've got booked for the next tour. Three nights at Wembley Arena. Which they'll probably move to the stadium."

He put his hand across his forehead, as if my very presence was giving him a blinding headache. "Why do you always have to be like that?" he growled.

"Oh God, forget it. This is enough bickering for one day. Can we please find somewhere to stay? I've got to sit down and have a Coke before we go to the show. I bet Dillon's having his sit-down and coke about now too." I patted the side of my nose. Thank the Lord, Ray managed to crack a smile.

We checked into a B&B, but quite an artsy one. There was a poetry reading that night. The poetry looked bad. The key to the room was a proper metal one, not a stupid plastic credit card like you get in big hotels. The bed was a double. Ray threw his coat over it, attempting to cover it, like he was dignifying a dead body. I studied myself in the bathroom mirror. My eyes were bigger than I remember, bigger and darker than they had been this morning in Ray's rearview mirror.

"Ray. Do you think I'm gross?"

"No, not at all," he called back, sniffing under his armpits for BO.

"I think I'm pretty."

"I think you are too. I just said so."

I put on some bronze-tinted Guerlain lip-gloss. "But am I pretty like a kid or pretty like a woman?"

"Did you say pretty or petty?"

I came out of the bathroom and kicked him.

We made tea in the room and then headed back out for Skyline. It was pouring rain and the kids were getting soaked. Like I said, Skyline attract a different kind of audience from Ray. They were all leering at me and pointing at Ray again, and I started to regret suggesting this excursion. The lads were whacking each other and pouring beer over each other's head and I felt pathetically intimidated. Being with Ray made me feel worse, as if everyone, especially the girls, was looking at me because I wasn't pretty enough to be out with a pop star. Of course, the big lunk chose that moment to put his arm around me and some men in anoraks whistled and started singing his songs. Why do people do that? Like Ray has never heard them before. He wrote the fucking things.

We had passes for the balcony, where we sat next to the band's manager and the guitarist's girlfriend, who I think I recognised from *I-D*, although I'm not *au fait* with the style magazines. Skyline sloped onstage at twenty past ten, by which time the crowd were beating each other up. I hardly even noticed when Dillon ambled onstage, tambourine in hand, so tiny was he. But as he crept up to the microphone, the crowd let out an almighty roar and the girls leaning over the front of the barriers began to faint.

The drummer rolled out a fucked-up marching-band beat and the bassist plucked out a fuck-you thwack. Then the guitar kicked in. It ground and shimmied around the room, as if it were a whole person in its own right, unattached to the person playing it. He was so skilled at his instrument that he made it sound like he had no control. Finally Dillon tipped his head back and opened his mouth as wide as a Muppet and began to sing. I realised immediately why he looked so tiny and insignificant. His voice was so huge that there was nothing left for the rest of him.

I couldn't believe I hadn't paid any attention at all to Dillon or Skyline. Here was a real white soul singer, as good as Rod, as good as Stevie Winwood, as good as anything in Manny's record collection. I was riveted. I didn't even look round to see what Ray was doing. I didn't know what the songs were called and I couldn't make out the words. But it felt like reading Truman Capote—it was so brilliant that you didn't even feel yourself taking it in. It was just in you, in one grace-ful swoop. Although they were whipping the crowd into a frenzy of pogoing and bear-hugging and glass-throwing, they sounded inexplicably elegant. The way this group played, they should have looked like Kristin Scott Thomas, not a gang of Liverpudlian drips. Their music seemed to rise, like smoke, to the ceiling. You could only look up at it. They played for barely an hour with no encore.

I was terrified to ask Ray what he thought, in case he dis-missed it as shit, but when Skyline went offstage, Ray was smiling. "Yeah, pretty good. The kid's got style, I'll give him that." But he didn't want to go backstage. And neither did I. When you see a band that great, you shouldn't try and go backstage and hang with them because by the end of the night, the experience will have lost its purity, from scrounging lights and sharing bottles of warm beer and making small talk. I was applying the same theory that Treena does to one-night stands. Great fuck? True romance? Then get the hell out of there before he wakes up, so you don't have to face the reality of bleary eyes, bad breath, and stubble.

When we got back to the room, I could hardly put the key in the door. My head was buzzing and my ears were ringing. It was one of the best shows I had ever seen. I've seen five—one of them was Elton John at Wembley Arena with Manny. I was writing a review in my head, considering buying space in the NME to print it as an advert. Ray went into the bathroom and began to brush his teeth. I pulled off my jeans and crawled into bed. I wondered where Dillon was and who he was with and what he was thinking and if he wanted to be there. I wondered what Drew thought of Skyline and Dillon, and I couldn't believe that it hadn't come up. So much I hadn't asked him. So much he hadn't told me. How could he not have told me that?

Ray came back into the room and flicked off the light. I heard him take his jumper off over his head and heard his elbows crack. I listened as his belt came undone and he kicked off his jeans. Then he gingerly eased himself under the covers. Although I couldn't see him, I knew he was turned away from me. He didn't talk but his breathing was very loud. I didn't know if I was supposed to notice it or not. I thought I felt a hairy knee brush past me.

"Ray, is that your foot?"

He threw back the covers. "Oh, for God's sake. I'll sleep on the floor."

"No, I didn't mean that."

But he lay down on the carpet and pulled the cover blanket over him, up to his nose.

"Well, I'll sleep there with you, then."

I cosied up to him and tried to get under his arm, but he turned away and huffed.

"Why won't you cuddle me?"

He pulled the cover over his head and lifted the side just enough so I could hear him. "Because you're in your knickers and you're a girl. I know you're just you, but men have reactions. You don't want to know."

"No, I don't." I pulled sharply away and ran to the bathroom. Oh God, he thought I was trying to . . . trying to do a Lolita.

How dare he be so presumptuous? How dare he think that?

I stormed back into the room. "Do you often think I'm trying to seduce you? Do I make you feel that uneasy? Because if you think that, then there's no point in us being friends. If I'm just another young girl you have to fend off."

"Please, Viva, don't be like that. But try to understand. I'm a bit drunk. And I'm a man. I've got a penis."

"You haven't, Ray. That's why I like you."

Sighing miserably to himself, he whipped it out. "There."

I looked at it in amazement. That's what all the fuss is about? It looked like such a rushed job, as if God hadn't had time to finish it properly. "Okay, Ray, I don't like you anymore."

He put it away. I got back into bed and closed my eyes tight, willing myself to fall asleep as quickly as possible. I don't know if Ray slept well, but when I woke up, he was staring at the ceiling.

TWELVE

Ray pulled his covers back, inch by inch, as if they were the wrapping on the last present of Christmas, on the last Christmas of his life. Try as he might, he couldn't help looking disappointed at what the wrapping contained. He was expecting something else, something bigger, someone else. Gingerly, he stood up and crept towards me and then peered from four feet away—close enough to see if I was awake, far enough to pretend he was looking at the clock on the night table. When he saw my eyes were open, he stopped looking. Manny always says that it's disrespectful to look at a dead body because it can't look back. My limbs felt very cold and heavy.

Ray put on his clothes and gathered up his bag without once glancing at me. I didn't take my eyes off him. It's always a shock when I see Ray for what he is—not some amorphous lump of Disney sexuality, but a rollicking, frolicking, wounded-pride Peckinpah woman-hater. In other words, a man. And, like a man, he was acting as if we had had sex with each other, when the whole point was, we hadn't. I wanted to jump on his back and make him carry me round the room until he said sorry. But with the mood he was in, he would have reported me for sexual harassment. If, as Gloria Steinem stresses, sexual harassment is not about sex but about power, I suppose his behaviour could be taken as a twisted compliment: he believed I had made sexual overtures to him because he felt I was stronger than him. However, in my heart, I knew he had put a sexual spin on us sharing a room, not because of any power struggle, but because he's vain. I wished he were Treena.

Treena runs around naked, but it isn't showing off. Half the time, she doesn't seem to realise that the knockout body is in any way attached to her. Now and then she'll catch a glimpse of herself in the mirror and hoot, "Well, will you look at those," and "Hot diggity! Nice ass, baby." She loves her looks but doesn't think about them, unlike most teenage girls, who dislike their looks but think about them all the time.

She's the only one in the gym changing-room who doesn't give a damn. Nobody looks at her anymore because they've seen it so many times now. I'm always fascinated by the shy girls who turn changing into their kit into an obsessive-compulsive sadomasochistic ritual. They take their knickers off without taking off their leotards, or put their T-shirts on before they take their school blouse off, so you never catch a glimpse of their bra. It's like watching a tropical fish trying to mate with itself at the bottom of the ocean.

Ray went into the bathroom. I heard him tinkle. I also heard the lock flick. Oh, wise precaution. Like I was going to burst in and plead, "Go on, Ray, let me watch you wee-wee." I made sure I was turned away from him when he unlocked himself and came huffing back in. I talked to the wall, which I noticed was fern green with a wood-panel border. I cleared my throat, like I was about to declare a new law.

"Morning, Ray. Sleep well?" He harrumphed and I kept

talking. "I'm going to get up in a minute and go to the hotel. I want to try and talk to anyone who might have seen Drew. That's why we came here, after all."

"Well, look," he answered, with the cool, steely tones of an outlaw, "I'm going to go back. I've just remembered that I have an appointment back in London. I'm meeting someone for lunch. Um . . ." I know he would have kept talking if he could think of anything else to say. He couldn't, so he tried to hustle me into a corner with his manly silence. I spun around to face it and it crashed over my body like a ten-foot wave on Zuma Beach. I swam forty-five degrees parallel to the shore so I wouldn't get dragged out to sea, coughing the salt water up and out of my lungs and trying to keep my swimsuit from getting ripped from my body.

"You just remembered you've got an appointment? Who are you meeting?"

"The girl I like."

"Oh." Now I felt as if we *had* done something the night before and that Ray was about to cheat on me. How I must bore him with my non-cocaine, no-sex-in-toilets lifestyle. How he must long for leggy models and hard drugs when I'm talking to him about Kubrick and Kafka. I always thought he was listening intensely, but now I see he was merely bored. Hotel rooms are funny things. They make everything look different. If people have to sleep with each other, sexually or platonically, they should do it in kitchens. The kitchen is the epicentre of truth in any home or building. You could never misconstrue a look or a word or a touch in the icy cool, compartmentalised presence of a fridge.

"How will I get home?"

He checked his woman's hair in the dirty bronze-framed mirror. "The train goes every half hour from the station. You're a big girl now. You don't need me to chauffeur you."

Well, for a start, I'm not a big girl and I never will be. If you don't get fat or tall by my age, it's unlikely you ever will. And, actually, I did need him to chauffeur me. I love being driven. It's the curse of the Springsteen fan who doesn't know how to drive. You're always going to have to seek out someone willing to cruise into Badlands with you with the top down and the radio blasting. To live Bruce's hymns to the independence of the open road can offer, the non-driver has to have a friend who knows how to work it. It's a tough call. You may find someone who will let you ride with them, but they'll probably be grumpy about driving with the top down and may well order you to take that Springsteen shit out of the tape-player.

I'm never going to learn to drive. I refuse to learn how to do anything I can't do naturally. In my head I'm such an accomplished and creative guitar player that I'm still surprised every time I pick up Manny's acoustic to find that I can't play at all. Not one note. That's why I hate French so much. God, I would love to open my mouth and be fluent, and I believe one day I will. But sitting down and learning how to form the words—it seems, somehow, like cheating.

Ray zipped his bag, closing, with it, the subject. Then he wrinkled his nose, mimed a gagging motion with his throat, and growled, "Since when do you wear perfume?"

I gathered the sheet around my neck. "I've always worn it."

"Well, it used to smell different. Light and girly." Bloody hell. "Light and girly!" He was, of course, describing his ideal woman: lightly sketched, in face and character, and very young-looking. He was in a total rage, as powerful as it was pointless. I looked up at him and his face was the colour of Paloma Picasso's mouth.

"Why?" he yelled. "Why do you suddenly smell like a French whore?" Then he walked out the door, slamming it like it was the new Skyline album. And all I could do was laugh. How does he know what a French whore smells like? You're so vain, you probably think this pong is about you. Calvin Klein got it wrong—he shouldn't have called his perfume "Escape . . . For Men," he should have called it "Escape . . . From Men." Then every sane woman in the Western world would buy twenty bottles.

It was only ten-thirty—another hour and a half before checkout. Knowing Ray, he would soon forget to settle the bill on his blaze through the front door. I'm sixteen and I'm always picking up the bill after Ray, who is twenty-six and a pop star. It's not that he's deliberately mean. It's just that he only ever has a million-pound note that he can't possibly break into. Luckily, I had my cheque book with me. I was incredibly proud when I first got it. Ray immediately mocked it, dubbing it "My First Cheque Book" because of the endangered animals of the world printed on each slip.

I was so angry. Straight men are absolutely disgusting, they really are. They're always jumping to the wrong conclusions, and picking their noses and farting, and they're always masturbating. Ray told me that when he's in the studio he sometimes does it seven times a day. He says that's nothing—Tommy told him he likes to masturbate over the backs of sleeping girls after he's had sex with them. Treena slept with a man who advocated male sex with melons. Once a week, he'd go down to the market in Portobello, buy a medium-sized melon, take it home, slice it in half, make a small hollow in the centre, and have sex with it. I have this perverse reaction whenever I know someone has a slant on me—I play up to it. If I think there's a girl at school whose family doesn't like Jews, I always make sure to offer her a bit of my bagel or to ask her if she wants to come see the new Woody Allen film with me. I think that's one way to make it clean again—to take it to such an extreme that everyone starts laughing. So if Ray wanted me to act like a sexpot, I would, even if he wasn't there to see it.

I took my underwear off and arranged myself in what I imagined to be a postcoital position. I thought postcoital thoughts, like "My, I feel so satisfied and inspired" and "Is he going to ring me?" and "Was that it?" But my mind kept wandering to who was my favourite character on *The Simpsons* and whether short hair makes a short person look taller or smaller. Treena later assured me that those are legitimate post-sex thoughts in her book, and that, since I asked, excessively long hair makes little people look dumpy.

When I got downstairs, reception was abandoned. It was like the bed-and-breakfast had become a ghost town overnight. I wanted to pay, but I was suddenly frightened—where was the woman we checked in with? Why had she been so insistent that we sign into her thinly used guest book? Why were all the mirrors so dirty?—and I walked out the door without looking back. I stopped momentarily, blinking in the sunlight, and fumbled in my Jackie O sunglasses. Scrambling to hook them over my ears, I ran, as fast as I could, up the side street and onto the promenade. It was incredibly blustery, and to get to the Metropole I had to cling to the railings beside the boardwalk and pull myself along as if I were on roller skates. The boys from the night before were throwing up in the gutter and crashed out on benches, even collapsed in heaps on the crappy pebble beach.

I swung through the revolving glass door of the Metropole, the hotel where Drew had last been seen, behind a business-man wearing a Stetson hat. He marched up to the bar and started complaining, in an undulating Texan accent, about the weather and how he had been assured it was going to be sunny this weekend. Assured by who? God? The girl behind the bar had pixie-cut red hair and big green eyes. She listened to him with ill-disguised boredom and he got even angrier. She pointed out the weather report from *The Times* and he shut up. "Weekend forecast: overcast." To Americans, the English *Times* is even bigger than God. Primly adjusting his hat like it was a tiara, he crept off to the lift. I sidled up and placed my hands on the maple between me and pixie-hair. My nail varnish was fucked. It was thick and gloopy, apart from the tips, where dirt glared unashamedly through, like a peeping Tom, unaware that it could be seen. We both gazed at my fingers disgustedly, forgetting briefly who and where we were. I moved my hands and her head snapped up.

"Yes? What can I get you?"

"Um, well actually, I just wanted to ask you something. A friend of mine went missing from this hotel a couple of weeks ago. We haven't seen him since. I was wondering if there was anyone who might have spoken to him that night? He was small and skinny, with longish dyed black hair and big brown eyes. He looked like Natalie Wood." She twitched when I asked her about Drew. I saw that he had touched her too.

"I don't know who Natalie Wood is," she laughed nervously, "but, yes, I remember the gentleman you're talking about. I heard that he disappeared. It's quite upsetting because," she paused, "we talked for quite a long time that night." Her eyes glazed over. "He was all wet. He had been swimming in the pool downstairs and his hair was in his eyes."

Drew had obviously been going around town, enticing young girls into his bedroom to talk about the situationists and Tennessee Williams. And they were never the same again.

"What did you talk about?"

"Oh. This playwright called Tennessee Williams."

"Really? Are you a fan?"

"Well, I wasn't before I met Drew. I hadn't heard of him. But after our talk, I read a little bit."

"Did you like it?"

She looked miserable. "Not really." A gust of wind spun through the revolving door. With tears in her eyes, she whispered, "I don't read much. I don't know why he picked me."

I didn't tell her the truth: because you were there; because you would listen. Instead I shrugged my shoulders, smiled forgivingly, and asked, "Did he say anything else?"

"He said a lot." She shook her head and mussed up her hair. "I can't remember it all. Something about some old movie star. You know, the one who's a bit like Johnny Depp but fat?"

"Marlon Brando?"

"Yeah, him. And he said something about how you should 'never allow yourself to feel anything, because the minute you do, you feel too much.' And that the male chromosome is just an incomplete female chromosome. And that he truly believes his life would have taken a different course if he had been born with blue eyes."

"Anything else?"

"He kept calling room service for more drinks."

"Okay. I get the picture. Thank you for your help."

I sat in the lobby for a little while with my head in my hands. I could ask anyone who'd ever met him if Drew had given them any clues in his conversation and they would all say the same thing: "Well, he mentioned Marlon Brando, Arthur Miller, Tennessee Williams, Judaism, and the futility of life past the age of fifteen." I guess Drew had a little spiel just like everybody else. Mine is "I'm just an insecure teenage Jew." His was "I just want to be an insecure teenage Jew." Throw in "anorexic," "alcoholic," "self-mutilator," and "death-wish," and you have Drew.

I was more convinced than ever that his death was merely a wish. Like all great wishes, the last thing he wanted was for it to come true. As a matter of course, I looked at the pool he had swum in, but it was just a pool. A pool with fat ladies in bathing caps doing the backstroke, small children surreptitiously weeing in the shallow end, and suspicious white-haired men hanging around the women's changing-room. There were no mysterious markings on the bottom of the pool, or bloodstains on the side, or a note attached to the drainage system saying, "I didn't jump off the bridge. I've gone to Iceland to stay with Bjork. Here's my address . . ."

That girl behind the bar was probably just as bowled over by him as I was. How could you spend an evening with Drew and not go home feeling traumatised? Ray was the only one who never paid him that much attention, the only one who wasn't bowled over by his beauty and genius. He had plenty of time to be won over—they toured together for weeks. But he remained resolutely unimpressed. Did that make Ray special or stupid? I thought Drew was the little boy in the Emperor's New Clothes, but maybe it was Ray all along.

With a heavy heart and a light backpack I walked to the station, trying to beat off the ferocious wind with a ferocious scowl. I couldn't go back to the pier. I would have been blown over the edge. I could hardly feel my fingers when I paid for my ticket. There was no point in paying since no conductor ever came through my carriage. Green-gilled boys dotted the rain, lolling with their heads against the windows, summoning their Thunderbird-tinged breath, every so often, to sing a snatch from a Skyline song.

Their hangovers deactivated them. They didn't laugh or jeer at me and I curled up with my legs on a spare seat and tried to sleep. The train took forever and I had to change at East Croydon—former home of Kate Moss and, judging by the lank-haired delinquents smoking on the platform, a variety of other surly girls. At Victoria Station I went into WH Smith to buy the *NME* and also ended up purchasing *In Style,* an offshoot of *People* magazine. It had Bette Midler and her beautiful Malibu loft house on the cover and twelve pages devoted to pictures of Sharon Stone in backless dresses. I spent the last of my cash on a cab home. I can't read in moving cars because it makes me feel sick. This is something I know from experience. But I did and I was and I'm sure I will again. Manny says that's the crucial difference between a neurotic and a psychotic: neurotics learn from their mistakes.

* * *

Manny didn't seem very pleased to see me. He had an egg-and-crabmeat soup stain on his pale blue silk blouse and toothpaste round his mouth. His new young friend, a student filmmaker called Keith, hadn't rung and they had last seen each other on Wednesday.

"Fuck him. Three days later is the cutoff date," I trilled, repeating what Treena had told me.

"How do you know?" he snapped. "You've never had a boyfriend."

We both blinked at each other for a few seconds. Then I cried and cried and Manny cried harder and begged me to forgive him. He was right, of course. I haven't ever had a boyfriend. I've had the Games teacher—my one great love— but that's different. And Manny doesn't know about him. Why tell him? It wouldn't exactly make me feel vindicated. And I knew, in my head, that that was probably the purest romance I'll ever be party to. Why turn the gleaming copper a mottled green by exposing it to the traffic fumes of the real world? Let it stay in my head and in my heart, tucked into a bed of song lyrics and film trivia.

Poor Manny. The cruelty with which he had addressed me made him shake and me feel very calm. There it is. Everyone has it in them. With Manny, at least it's a surprise. It upsets me more when Treena does it because I expect it of her. I practically will her to be mean. And when she is, I remember how formulaic the world is. You can only dodge the rules for so long. If you look like Treena does, you're supposed to act like a little bitch. That's the truth. Like Manny taught me, it is one's duty to judge a book by its cover. It makes understanding your own role in life a lot easier. I can't get away with as much as Treena because I'm not as pretty. Life will be harder for me. But I will also get more out of it. I don't kid myself. Maybe one day I will wake up walking and talking like a tall blond cheerleader and that will be the first day of the rest of my life.

Everyone was starting to sound like the girls at school. Ray had been an unbearable bitch all weekend and now Manny too. It was an epidemic. These were the people I had surrounded myself with in order to combat the jerks in my class. My force-field shield had a tear in it. Strangely, the student body were less offish with me than anyone I talked to all week. Stacey Lyttle lent me her ink eradicator and Helen Barton-West let me eat two of her Minstrels.

School itself was becoming a colossal drag. Lessons dragged on so pathetically. I thought they'd collapse before they reached the end. In double Biology, I watched the clock so hard it started to move backwards and then I had no choice but to get on with my work. At least I tried to. You can say "Okay, let's get to work" as much as you like, but that doesn't mean it gets done. I was thinking all these positive thoughts, chanting educational mantras, but it made not a jot of difference. I still don't understand the question.

That Nike advert is such a crock. "Just do it." I try so hard to do "it," but "it" seems only to encapsulate the tasks of eating too many crisps, watching *Seinfeld*, spending money I don't have on things I don't want, and drawing Montgomery Clift's face on my hand. It's like, I love the idea of carrots, but not enough to actually eat them. I love the idea of knowing about history. I sit there thinking, "God, this is so great. I'm going to know all about Italian unification. That really is fascinating." And I spend so long imagining how much I'll know by the end of the lesson that, when the bell rings, I haven't heard a single word the teacher's said.

On Monday after my journey to Brighton, Treena was all psyched up, revising for the RS exam, our very last GCSE. I hate it when she does that. It's like she snaps, for no reason. She never warns me she's going to do it. Psychos shouldn't get psyched about anything. They should just *be*. A psycho with a cause is no fun at all. I don't know how she does it because she is hardly an incandescent mind. Still, she can cook when she wants to. She is, when she feels like it, perfectly capable of sewing back a button that has come off a coat. She knows how to work the computer in the library. What it comes down to is that we are differently brained.

I looked for her in the dining room, but she wasn't anywhere to be seen, and the dinner lady told me the box of Toffee Crisps was still at a healthy level, so I knew she couldn't have hit the snack counter yet. After checking the changing-rooms and banging on a few toilet doors, I found her at a table at the back of the library, leaning against the radiator. She had her folder spread open in front of her and was chewing on a pen that had a naked lady on it. The librarian was on patrol, throwing out anyone who was using her church to chatter, read *Just Seventeen*, or deal acid. I tried to pass Treena a note but she wouldn't take it. I kicked her leg and she exhaled sharply.

"What, Viva? I've got a lot to do." Yeah, right. She only has ten fingers and ten toes. How long could it take to paint twenty nails?

"Sorry, Treena. It's just . . . I still don't understand about the roots of Islam. Do you want to work on it together? You can come to my house after school."

She began affixing white binding rings to each page of work in her folder. "Can't you work it out for yourself? You're supposed to be the smart one."

Yeah, I thought, I am supposed to be the smart one. Get off my turf. I felt my cheeks flush and was gripped by the nauseating sense that Treena, once again, held a flush deck. I wish she'd tell me when we're playing. Not even having a pack of cards to play with does make me feel as if I'm somewhat at a disadvantage. My legs started to tingle and I began to feel a little faint. I opened the wrought-iron window opposite the table and took deep breaths from the pit of my stomach, which had housed so many different brands of chocolate over the last few days, it was becoming a kind of safe house for unwanted confectionery. I provide sanctuary for out-of-date Kit Kats that would otherwise end up on the streets. Treena stood up and slammed the window shut. The clatter reverberated around the hushed room. In a flash of comfortable footwear, the librarian was beside us.

"She closed it," I sulked.

"She opened it," hissed Treena, giving me the evil eye.

"She stuck gum behind the radiator and ripped a page out of an Evelyn Waugh book for no reason other than she thinks he has a silly name."

The librarian's eyes blazed. She looked like a Quentin Blake illustration in a Roald Dahl book. "Did you do this, Katerina?"

"Yes." She rolled her eyes. "A year ago."

The librarian couldn't have been more upset than if she had caught us using the library to have tattooed heroin sex with members of Mötley Crue. She looked like she might cry. "You find Evelyn Waugh amusing?"

"Well, not him, strictly. His name." Treena sighed, really not wanting to go into it. "It's a girl's name."

I interjected. "Not just that, it's a creepy girl's name."

The librarian slammed the table with her hands. "Evelyn Waugh is not a laughing matter. Although you might find, if you took the time, that his writing is very funny indeed. Katerina, you will scrape that gum off after school."

I burst out laughing and they both glared at me. I tried and tried, but I couldn't stop and was, to my enormous relief, thrown out.

I cut afternoon lessons and went into town, attempting to adjust my uniform so it didn't look like I was skipping school. I pulled my tie, shirt, and grey wool tights off and wore my white vest and bare legs. I looked weird and felt cold. Placing myself by the coat stand in Patisserie Valerie, I wolfed down a cappuccino and a book of Truman Capote short stories. They're stories and they're short and they're by him. Bliss. I ordered a vegetarian club sandwich because I thought it sounded healthy. But when the waitress set it in front of me, I saw it involved no actual vegetables, just a lot of different types of cheese and some celery.

I picked each piece of celery out because celery takes up more calories to chew than it actually contains and is therefore an even bigger waste of time than *Eyes Wide Shut*. So I ordered what I really wanted, which was a hot chocolate and a slice of cheesecake. As I plunged my fork into the glutinous yellow cake, I studied the people at the other tables. There were a lot of Japanese girls with Vivienne Westwood carrier bags and dyed hair. If Ray were here, he would say, "There's a nasty Nip in the air." He's anti-Semitic too, although he doesn't quite know it.

When Manny took me to New York last time, Ray asked me, "What's your family there like? What do they do? I bet they're all diamond merchants." He referred to one journalist as a "fucking Irish potato-head." Apart from the "nasty Nips," there was a harassed-looking woman reading the *Guardian* and an old lady with pale lilac hair and no eyebrows. She was eating a broccoli quiche. I know because she told everyone: "I am eating a quiche. It has broccoli in it." I was moderately interested.

I got talking to a nice gay couple from San Francisco, because they noticed I was now reading *Breakfast at Tiffany's*. The elder lover had receding peroxide hair and the young one I don't really recall too much about, other than that I fancied him and might have fallen in love with him if he hadn't taken wild offence at something I said and stopped talking to me entirely. Here it is: for a joke, I pronounced Truman Capote's name the wrong way. They looked at me, and then at one another, and then they just got up and left, without even tipping the waitress. I am self-destructive. Everyone says so. I'm always mispronouncing words I know how to say perfectly well so that everyone will think I'm dumb and laugh at me and hate me forever.

I went to Boots and messed with samples and the lady behind the counter shouted at me because I put eyeliner straight from the pen to my lids. "You're supposed to test it on the back of your hands!" she screamed, as if eye/pen contact could only result in a drawn-out death. So I had a big thick black trail on one eye and not the other. Why should I test it on my hand? What good is it to me there? I adjourned to the Estée Lauder stand and sprayed a lot of different perfumes on my wrist until I smelled so disgusting I believed I would throw up if I didn't rip my own skin off within three seconds. I pulled and pulled, but my skin stayed on my arms.

And then, because I was there and not in History, I decided to watch a film. Having seen every movie playing in the West End, I had no option but to buy a ticket for *The Crow: City of Angels 2*. It was awful, and I sat there thinking, "Why am I by myself in an empty cinema at four in the afternoon?" I left before the end and went directly home, without passing Go, where I slammed the door behind me and retired to my boudoir. I was dressing up as Elizabeth in *The V.I.P.s*, with a pencil skirt, cream angora sweater, fat lady's coat, flesh-coloured stockings with a black seam, and a snood, when the phone rang.

I wasn't at all surprised to hear from Ray that night. Whenever he's a pig, he always rings me after a couple of days and chats as if nothing has happened.

"Oh. Hello. How was your lunch date?"

He started speaking all fast and bubbly and difficult to understand, like an MTV VJ. "It was great. She was fucking great. I think you'd approve. She's really cool, really sorted. She's a bit like you."

"But tall and blond?" I cooed, viciously. He laughed. I didn't. "Well, Ray, you seem to have chippered up. I thought, after Brighton, you were never going to speak to me again."

"Yes, I'm sorry about that. I was just having a bit of a funny turn. I'm fine now."

"Oh, how marvellous, because I'm fucking miserable." I held the phone away from me and made a face at it.

"Don't be sad." I heard his voice, like a tiny fairy at the bottom of the garden. "I'm so happy. I don't want you to be unhappy. I've really got my head in a good place."

I pressed the receiver to my mouth. "What, at the top of your neck?"

He ignored me. "I've got an idea. Can I come round?"

I carried the receiver out into the landing and yelled down the stairs, "Manny, can Ray come over?"

Manny waved a hand above my head, like "Sure, whatever." He doesn't fancy Ray and is, more to the point, unimpressed by him, although "Ray is certainly very impressed with himself." He doesn't think Ray's glamorous enough to be my friend: "There's a difference between being working-class and being common, and Ray, I'm afraid, is the latter." Manny adores Treena—"She has the most wonderfully shaped head"—and I can tell he is, against his better judgement, rather intrigued by Drew.

Ray brought fish and chips and we sat around the dinner table listening to his big plan. He was wearing a baggy grey polo-neck jumper and three days of growth. He and Manny drank a bottle of red wine and I had a Sprite. When Manny went to the kitchen for an ashtray, I tested how sorry Ray was about being mean by making him open my Sprite for me—he did it without flinching—and getting him to check my nose for snot. I tilted my neck back and he peered up my nostrils. "All clear, darlin'."

"Are you sure? It feels itchy."

He put his arm round the back of my chair and kissed my cheek. "Right, what I've come to say is, I'm going to America to do promo next week."

I wiped my nose. "Yeah? So?"

"They're releasing the second album on a new label who are much more supportive. And the record company here has given me a bonus because the album's gone platinum. They've given me ten thousand pounds to play with, as holiday money. I was thinking, since you finish school next week, that you could come with me. They're putting me in the Chateau Marmont for five days. I'll pay for your flight and your room and you could even bring a friend, so you don't get bored when I'm doing all the MTV promo and that."

My guard was somewhat up because this I know about my one male friend: Ray can be a very sweet boy, but mostly when he doesn't think too hard about it. And this all sounded suspiciously well thought out. But I was deliriously happy. My highs are so high and my lows are so low. Get out of school and go straight to L.A.? Yes, thank you so much. I plonked myself in his lap and tucked his hair behind his ears. "Why are you doing this?"

"Because I know you're going to do that Religious Studies exam brilliantly. And I want you to have a reward. I don't do enough for you. You're my kid sister and I don't like to see you hung up on . . . life."

Manny came back into the room. "You mean hung up on this Drew person?"

"Yes, that especially. I don't want you to think about it anymore. Or any more than you need to. Be a kid. Have some fun. Go shopping on Melrose. Share a swimming pool with Jack Nicholson."

"Jack Nicholson's definitely going to be in my swimming pool?"

"Well, whoever. Someone like him. It is California." He laughed nervously, fearful I was missing the point.

"Okay, someone like him, so does that mean Roman Polanski or Warren Beatty?"

Manny sighed as he poured himself another glass of wine. "Well, Warren Beatty is now a happily married man with many delightful children. I'm sure he lives on a ranch in Vermont. And it's not going to be Roman Polanski because he's banned from entering the country."

"Yeah, he's right." I sounded suspicious.

"Look," wailed Ray, tugging at his sleeves, "we'll be in a great hotel. I'm getting the full treatment. Proper pop-star stuff. At some point, I swear to God, there will be a movie star in your swimming pool."

"A proper one? Not just some chick from *Dawson's Creek*?"

"Yes."

"You promise?"

"I promise."

I jumped up. "Okay then, I'll go."

"Well, I think it's an excellent idea," Manny said, smiling. Then he sipped from his glass, one eyebrow raised in an arch as curly as the writing on a Coke can.

Ray was like an excited little kid at a birthday party who had just been told he could help the birthday girl blow out the candles. "It will be brilliant. You could take anyone you want. You can take Treena. I have to go on Monday, but I've got you two tickets leaving on Thursday so you don't miss any school. I've got a day in New York, a day in Boston, and then I get to Los Angeles the same day as you. I'll pick you up at the airport and we'll go to the hotel together."

I popped a soggy chip into my mouth and picked up the phone. The vinegar mingled with my growing excitement. "Treena, do you want to go to Los Angeles on Thursday? Ray's paying."

"Yeah, okay."

I hopped triumphantly from leg to leg and did a little bear dance as I slammed down the phone. "Treena says, 'Yeah, okay.'" In my experience, slamming down the phone is an act best employed and most enjoyed when you're very happy. If someone really angers you during the course of a telephone conversation, you should hang up very slowly and calmly, without saying another word. That always gets them. I've done it to Manny twice and Ray a couple of times. It's not worth doing it to Treena because she wouldn't notice. She barely knows what a phone is. Half the time I have to yell, "Treena, you're speaking to the wrong end. Try again."

It was after Ray had gone home, as Manny lay on his bed reading a book about the socialist symbolism in Hollywood musicals, and as I soaked in the bath, that I began to wonder why, even for her, Treena had sounded so underwhelmed. The next day at school she said I had just caught her in the middle of her revising and of course she was excited. She was just so worried about the RS exam. Like, hello, get a grip. It's Religious Studies. Who cares if you don't remember lines from the Bible? God's so fucking lazy, he just gave dictation, rambling, freaking out about floods and locusts. God must be really, really rich for the guys who had to type up his words not to call him on his self-indulgence. I wonder if God can get into the VIP room at the Met Bar?

When final exam day came, I found I had spent all week packing and consequently had no time whatsoever to revise. Ray's plan backfires again. Reward schemes are never very successful with me. Manny tried to potty-train me by buying a doll that wets itself and giving it a treat when it did its business on the potty. The treat was a packet of Smarties. When I saw them, I got so excited I wet myself. This was a somewhat similar situation.

I didn't care. Everyone else spent the morning recess hunched over their desks, desperately trying to cram in some last-minute information. I danced about the classroom doing the Jets dance from *West Side Story*. I felt sad that I was letting Drew down, but not so sad that I had to stop dancing. Treena was slumped in the back of the room with one hand over her eyes and the other holding open the textbook. Her eyes moved furiously across the page and she traced the words with her finger. The contents of her pencil case were spread before her. She had two erasers, a rule, a bottle of Tippex, pencils so sharp they looked like Susan Faludi's mind, and extra ink cartridges for her fountain pen. I remember when she bought that Tippex. It was so she could paint the heels of her Doc Martens white.

The exam went great. In terms of failing heroically, I can think of nothing more humiliating than almost passing. That's something I feel very strongly about. I once got 49 percent in a Maths exam, and I just wanted to die. So I glanced briefly through the paper, reached the conclusion that I was not going to do well, and opted to do very, very badly instead. I answered a few questions, and those I did were written with my left hand so that the writing was so slanted it could barely be read. It was a laborious and rewardingly pointless act. When the bell went and I was still only one quarter of the way through, I felt a huge sense of relief. There, I did the best I could do, just not in the way they expected me to. I'd be surprised if I even got 10 percent.

Treena seemed worried. She stayed behind to talk to the teacher and said I didn't have to wait. So I didn't.

I skedaddled home and started making the final sundress selection. Yes: pale blue one in the Eve Arnold photo of Marilyn Monroe brushing her hair in a public toilet. Yes: cherry-printed Marilyn cocktail outfit from *The Misfits*. No: white, full-skirted Elizabeth Taylor in *Cat on a Hot Tin Roof*. There was no way that dress would survive the ten-hour flight without *molto* crumpling.

I took three different pairs of sunglasses, six pairs of underpants (three of which were black and lacy and the rest were plain white with high waistbands). I put a bottle of sunblock in a travel bag and a few pieces of costume jewellery. Then Manny came and checked my packing and pointed out everything I had forgotten, like toothpaste and toothbrush, bras, trousers, T-shirts, shorts, and shoes. The next day Manny and I rose at 6:30 A.M. I put on a purple tweed dress, black ballet slippers, and big dark glasses, and he drove me to the airport, where we met Treena, who was wearing jeans and a hangdog expression. I had come as Jackie Kennedy. She had come as Jackie Mason. Despite her unusually dishevelled appearance, we got bumped up to first because the tickets had been booked through the record company.

The check-in attendant and passport control kept requesting that I remove my glasses so they could match me to my picture. My passport photo was taken when I was thirteen. I don't know if I had flu that day, or if the photographer shouted out an obscene suggestion at the moment he pressed the shutter, but it really does not look like me. My nose is wide and squashed. My smile is this horrible crooked slash with three old ladies' teeth sticking out over my bottom lip. My cheeks are all puffy. The only orderly thing in the frame is my hair, which is a perfect triangle of frizz. I look like Barbra Streisand. After a stroke.

They looked at me suspiciously when they checked my passport like I was taking the piss—no one could be that ugly. But I wasn't distraught because I knew the hideousness of the photo was only exacerbated by how pretty I looked in the flesh. I didn't want to take my glasses off entirely because I wanted people to think I might be a young film star on my way to a meeting with Billy Wilder, who was coming out of retirement for me. I'd just flip my glasses onto my forehead when they asked me, and sigh because I didn't want to have bloodshot eyes for the test shots.

As we boarded the plane, we saw Antonio Banderas skip up the staircase, wearing a dark grey linen suit and pale loafers. I make a point not to get infatuated with any film star who still has a healthy career, but him I love. He reminds me so much of the old-fashioned Latin lovers that he might as well have died in 1962. And he's so very beautiful that you wouldn't even want to have sex with him. There would be no point; it would be like virtual-reality sex. You'd be looking down on yourself, unable to feel a thing. But I wanted to look at him up close, just kind of have half an hour to peer at him.

Ten minutes into the flight, the stewardess brought us each a packet of pretzels and a glass of champagne. Within about three sips I was blasted and decided to write Antonio a letter explaining why he should let me interview him for my school magazine, although I wasn't certain that we had one. It started off quite plausibly: "I am a student at Griffins School for Girls in London. I know that you must be incredibly busy, but I was wondering if there was any chance that I could interview you for my school paper. It would be a real scoop!" Then I added three more exclamation marks for luck and because English is not his first language. And then I put upside down exclamation marks at the front of every sentence because I thought I'd seen that in a Spanish dictionary.

But by the third paragraph I was scribbling: "¡¡¡So anyway, I'm not an actual jet-set chick—I got bumped up to first!!!! I am drunk on free champagne so I feel it's okay to tell you that you are the most beautiful man in modern cinema. Some people think I look Latin, although really I'm Jewish!!! I like your suit. Is it linen? How is the kid you had with Melanie Griffith? I'm sorry her career has faded. ¡¡¡I thought she was great, especially in *Something Wild*. Please send her my love."

I handed it to the stewardess and told her that my friend Mr. Banderas was sitting in the upstairs deck and could she give him this note from me? Treena begged me not to do it. "It's a long flight. What if he shouts at us? What if he tells you to fuck off? Then we'll have to feel awful for ten whole hours."

"What, he's going to tell me off for saying he's handsome and has a lovely wife?"

She huffed and started flicking through the in-flight entertainment guide. I watched her pretend to read. Her eyes weren't as vivid as usual. They used to be emerald green, and now they looked more like spinach. I wondered if she could still see me properly through them. There was an outbreak of tiny red bumps across her forehead and her cheeks glistened with an oily film. Her brows were overplucked, too skinny at the front and straggly at the outer ends.

I never pluck my eyebrows unless I have something very serious to worry about, and then I use the pain to help concentrate my thoughts. She must have been thinking about something, although she had chosen not to share it with me. Which doesn't shock me. Treena doesn't really have a whole lot to share: she just is. It's very straightforward, but that means it's awfully hard to tell when something's amiss. She had definitely lost weight. All the lunch breaks that she should have spent eating Toffee Crisps in the canteen, she had spent hunched over her work in the library. I tried to remember the last time I had heard her get really excited about anything. It was a good two weeks, which may not sound like that long, but it is. Treena's favourite word is "amazing."

The stewardess came back and said, "I don't mean to be funny, but is Mr. Banderas really your friend? Because he seemed rather confused by your note."

Oh, God. I curled up into my chair. Why am I such an idiot? Stupid, stupid me. Stupid Antonio for getting freaked out by a little girlie love letter. We heard nothing more and I spent the rest of the flight putting a hex on his career. We were free to stand up and walk around the plane, so I meandered around the cabin and cursed it. I was glad the curtains were drawn so I didn't have to look at the poor people in business class. I plunked myself back into my seat and pushed a couple of buttons until it turned into a bed at least as comfortable as my one at home. But I was plagued by visions of Antonio calling ahead to his agent to let all of Hollywood know that a strange and uncool person was about to land in their country. I took solace in my complimentary travel kit, which contained, amongst other things, an aromatherapy facial spray and a tub of juniper eye cream. There was even a sofa in first, with a coffee table stacked with the new editions of *Vanity Fair* and *Vogue* and vibrantly coloured American candy and bottles of booze.

I nudged Treena. "See that table? I dare you to put that bottle of champagne in your hand luggage."

She didn't look up from the magazine. She appeared to be engrossed by the play list for the country music station. "No."

She still didn't look up. I grabbed the magazine from her hands and hissed, "Dolly Parton, Kenny Loggins, Garth Brooks. Now will you put it down and go steal me a bottle of champagne?"

"I can't. It's against the Lord."

"It's what?"

"Against the Lord."

"You mean against the law." It still amazes me how many expressions Treena has gone through her life completely mishearing, without any qualms and without anyone correcting her. I guess if someone's as pretty as she is, you want them to be right.

"Whatever."

"Look, it's not against the law. Everything here is free. If we don't take it, some fat fucker will. You have no qualms about stealing chocolate from family newsagents, or clothes from market stalls. Those people work for a living. This is an airline. We are in first class. These people are super-rich. It's fine."

"No."

So I did it myself. The stewardess saw me and actually smiled as I tucked the bottle into my bag.

It felt like we had swopped places. Maybe I am more powerful and daring than Treena, but only in airports and above oceans. Maybe her charisma vanishes outside Camden. Let me think. No, I've been very impressed with her in West London too. She had simply changed. It was as if the exam questions had scuttled up the pen as she wrote and run all the way up her arm and into her brain, never to loosen their grip. They crawled across her body like a plague of tiny ants. She bored me. I worried about spending a whole week with her, and already cursed her in my head for leaving wet towels on the floor, which she surely would, and for not wanting to play Twister at one in the morning, which two weeks ago would have been unlikely. But that was before her eyes turned the colour of spinach.

Imagine if Tommy Belucci suddenly became more famous and successful than Ray. He wouldn't like it. I felt the same way. The most exciting city in the most exciting country in the world and I was with the wrong person, or rather it had all been a terrible case of mistaken identity. In Camden, I could never have imagined a more right person to be with—to do anything with: to walk with me to the corner shop, to hold my hand on a trip to the moon. In a flash it suddenly occurred to me that if I had to spend one more minute with this person, I would actually fall on the floor from boredom.

As the plane descended into LAX, I felt like a maraschino cherry being dropped onto a bed of whipped cream. Every nervous, insecure, kvetchy pore in my body was genuinely jubilant and to hell with Treena and Antonio. The horrible bit is when you've landed but they won't let you off, they just keep circling the runway. I hate looking at food after I've finished it. No matter how much there is still left on my plate, I have to have it out of my sight. Sitting strapped into your seat on the plane ten minutes after it's landed is like that times ten. Finally, we were allowed to unbelt. I gathered up my bags and clipped back my hair, which had had a total hysterical attack and was pining for its real mommy, Art Garfunkel. As we disembarked from the plane, Antonio Banderas came up and asked which one of us was Viva. His eyes were so shimmery they looked gold. His skin was so gold it looked shimmery.

"Me," I stammered, swishing my hair like Stevie Nicks swishes her skirts.

"You're a smart girl. That was a smart note you sent over. I'll do an interview if I get a break in filming. You're staying at the Chateau? I'll ring you there. I'll send Melanie your love."

I completely stopped breathing for the walk through the terminal. In fact, I don't recall inhaling at all until someone rolled a trolley over my foot as I waited by the luggage carousel. Treena seemed angry at me. All through Customs she sighed and tutted and moaned about the wait for our baggage. Like it was my fault. She only mellowed when we hooked up with Ray, who was waiting with a big sign that said "Los Angeles welcomes Treena and Viva!!" Exclamation marks, I thought to myself. He must be happy. Hey, it worked for Antonio. Still, nothing remotely Dostoevskyan about that message.

I could tell this trip was destined to be the exclamation express. Good: I don't understand the correct use of all the other punctuation symbols. Here's a colon, have an apostrophe—take them, they're only cluttering up my room. An exclamation mark is a good bet and a kind friend, if one that you can never bring yourself to inform that she has been wearing, for the past eleven years, an eye shadow entirely unsuitable for her complexion.

Ray gave us both a big hug. He looked great, I have to say. In Los Angeles, his woman's hair was positively macho. The stubble on his chin was an inch past itchy and a centimetre before beard. His nose looked fine and aquiline. The last time I saw him it looked like it had got bored of being a nose and opted to become a root vegetable halfway through and without getting planning permission. He was wearing a white V-neck T-shirt and combat trousers. His broad, hirsute arms gave him the appearance of a tamed ape. He had a pleasant bouncy air about him, as if he were a space-hopper from the seventies and we should feel free to climb on his shoulders whenever we felt the urge.

He took our bags and led us to an enormous stretch limo with tinted windows. I asked if I could sit in the front. The seats were soft grey leather and there were two mobile phones. The chauffeur told us we could listen to any station we wanted and we chose Classic Rock. The first song we heard as we roared along the freeway was "Jump" by Van Halen and I felt desperately, stomach-churningly joyful. In London the streets are paved with gold. In Los Angeles the right songs play at the right moments. I looked in the rearview mirror. Treena had nodded off with her head on Ray's shoulder. He absent mindedly stroked her corkscrew curls. They have such gleaming hair, I thought dreamily. They should get married and have gleaming-haired children.

Van Halen turned into Aerosmith, Aerosmith into Oasis, Oasis into the Rolling Stones, the Stones into Aretha Franklin, Aretha into Springsteen, and as the Chateau came into view, the first terrible, beautiful chords of "Boys of Summer" cut through the limo like an unstoppable, spherical tear ruining a supermodel's eye makeup. As pleased as I was to be at the hotel, I did not want to get out of that car. I sat there in the front seat, looking at the L-shaped building with its canopies and balconies as Ray woke Treena up and they started carrying our bags into the lobby. Maybe they were being kind, maybe they had forgotten about me, but they just let me sit there. Finally, the driver opened my door. I looked up at him with pleading eyes, desperate to hear the last few notes. He held out his hand and I had to take it.

The Chateau Marmont is the most beautiful hotel in the world, part Greta Garbo, part Edgar Allan Poe. It is fancy, but not aggressively so, not like those hip New York hotels that practically knock you to the ground and kick minimalism in your face. I hate the idea of paying hundreds of dollars for a room and then not being able to find a light switch. At the Chateau, a light switch is a light switch, but better and more elegant than any light switch you've ever seen before.

It is the last of old Hollywood. Harry Cohn told William Holden, "If you must get into trouble, do it at the Chateau Marmont." Shelley Winters honeymooned there. It was also the place her new husband began an affair with Anna Magnani. Manny Hawks used to rent a room with views directly over the pool so he could ogle the bathing belles. You still see loads of starlets lounging by the pool. They have pale skin, pink sunglasses, small, pert breasts, and dainty tattoos on their ankles. You get a better class of B-movie aspirant at the Chateau.

The Chateau Marmont was the main reason I wanted to go to L.A. Manny had given me a book on its history and I'd slept with it under my pillow until I got a stiff neck. There's photos of Robert Mitchum doing the washing up and of Christopher Walken and Dennis Hopper slumped in leather chairs, looking like they are made out of wax. The Chateau has a luscious garden where you can eat breakfast, an enormous gym, a creaky little elevator, and a swimming pool surrounded by bungalows. The best room is a little house that sits at the top of a flight of stairs cut into the rockery. It is so meditative and relaxing to sit at the top of the stairs. Imagine how it must feel to sit at the top of the stairs, in a house at the top of the stairs. If I could stay there, I would be able to plan the rest of my life. One day it will be mine.

This was all stored in my head long before I even got to the airport. So there I was and I found I was reluctant to go in, in case it didn't live up to my expectations. I needn't have worried. The first thing I saw was a beautiful wooden magazine rack, stacked with *Interview* and imported copies of *The Face* and, even better, *Daily Variety* and the *Hollywood Reporter.* The magazine rack was beautiful. The magazines were beautiful. The plush lounge seated funny-looking best-supporting actors and women studio executives, talking in deep voices, drinking tea and looking glamorous. I was in heaven. If we are all made in God's image, I think the fair swap should be that heaven be made to our design. Tommy Belucci would spend the hereafter living in Pete Townshend's nose. Manny would spend it nestled in Elizabeth Taylor's cleavage. I would pluck my harp from the top of that magazine rack.

I decided it was a magic rack and would make my fame and fortune. I touched it softly with one finger and batted my eyelids. Here I was in a hotel populated by casting directors and Hollywood legends and I was trying to look alluring for a pile of magazines. Queuing in front of us was a girl from *Dawson's Creek.* Then we saw someone else.

THIRTEEN

"I don't believe it," spat Ray, dropping his bag on his feet.

I lifted up my glasses. "Wow, what a coincidence. Dillon from Skyline."

Ray kicked his bag across the lobby. "I walk in here, I see the girl from *Dawson's Creek,* and then I see that cunt. Why does he always have to spoil everything?"

"Who's Dillon from Skyline?" whispered Treena. She knew who he was—we'd discussed him and her exact words were "I wouldn't kick him out of bed"—so I don't know why she said that. Ray cracked a tiny smile and kissed the top of her head.

I looked at Dillon, revelling in his burgeoning fame, ordering his publicists around, and chatting up the receptionist. Dillon's anorak was zipped up to his chin, which is worse than not taking off your hat or not closing your umbrella indoors. I would kick him out of bed. Look at that washed-out face; he'd take up all the covers and snore and his feet would smell nasty from football practice.

Dillon didn't see us, surrounded as he was by an entourage of scousers and effusive, Armani-suited backslappers. Skyline's latest single had gone Top 10 in the *Billboard* charts. Their album was at number 9. They were being lauded as the first British band to break America since Depeche Mode. Negotiating his way through the mass of suits eager to extend their support, he ducked and bobbed, shadow-boxing with himself, which was odd, since there were so many actual men who would have been happy to be whacked if he had decided he wanted to punch them. They would have grinned and cried, "Good punch, Dillon!" before collapsing on the floor.

The hotel staff seemed a little wary of their hyper young guest and treated him with the same gritted-tooth reverence as they would the irritating child of a Saudi millionaire. "If there's anything at all we can do to make your stay with us more enjoyable . . ."

Ray was in for a harder slog. His album was at number 98 in the *Billboard* charts, which is not as bad as it sounds. The record company was sure that, with a little promotion, they could get it up to 88, then 64, and who knows? It might just take off. A record can hang around the lower regions of the American charts for a year becoming a hit. But he couldn't afford, as Dillon could, to sneer at the Yankee dollar, or refuse to play with the marketing director's children. Ray had hours and hours of regional radio interviews to do. There could be no illusion of Dostoevskyan cool, not if he wanted to break Minneapolis. He had to talk to teen magazines about his ideal babe and whether he preferred flat-chested girls to busty ones. He had to be third support on the bill to someone playing an out-of-town enormodome, which meant going onstage at half past two in the afternoon. He had to taste the food with an amateur chef on a cable channel and have his photo taken with extras from *Baywatch*.

People were polite to him because they weren't really sure who he was. He tried to help carry his bags to the bungalow and the bellboy kind of sneered at him, because it was less cool to make a big fuss about feeling guilty than to just let it go. Acting lowly makes you look lowly. Manny always says, "Don't tell yourself you're a dog. You're not, but it won't take long to convince everyone around you, if that's what you want them to think." Ray was in a bungalow next door to where John Belushi died and we were in a bungalow across the way, next to the Red Hot Chili Peppers, who played music all night long and lit candles around the swimming pool.

You think a hotel room is a bed and a desk until you've stayed at the Chateau. The bed was big enough to sleep four. The bathroom had tiles the exact colour of a mouse's ear. There might even have been mice, which added to the thrill. Obviously there weren't but the decor suggested it was a possibility. Polished antique furniture was scattered around the living room, complementing the high-tech electronic equipment. The TV had a sixty-inch screen and a video. The stereo had a CD-player with six different decks. The minibar had Hershey's Kisses and blue corn chips. I am a shallow person, but I felt so calm, like this is where I belong. In a hotel room with a VCR and blue corn chips. The record company had left us a vast welcoming basket containing fruit you could actually eat and not just look at. We took a bite from everything. We tried all the complimentary soaps, shampoos, and moisturizers. Then we said good night to Ray and collapsed into bed.

It was hot so we slept in our knickers and bras. Treena doesn't need to wear a bra because when she lies down her breasts stay exactly where they were. No one ever told them they're supposed to flop, so they don't. She had one leg kicked over the cover. Her snores scuttled across the bed like crabs.

I was absolutely shattered, but still, I woke up in the middle of the night because every inch of my body was so on alert for fun. My scalp tingled with anticipation of adventure. Is that the noise of someone from an Aaron Spelling miniseries throwing up? Does that sound like an infamous alternative-rock band jamming? I looked over at Treena, but she wasn't there. I worried for a few minutes, then decided she was probably having a midnight swim. I thought I heard someone in the water, splashing and spitting. I padded to the living room, peered through the curtains, and saw a slender dark figure climbing out of the pool. I sat in front of the television for a while, waiting for her to come in, but I fell asleep on the sofa. I didn't hear her creep back.

I don't know why I didn't ask her about it the next day, other than when I woke up I didn't really care. Ray had interviews until five, and gave us a hundred dollars each to amuse ourselves. If he had been any other man, I wouldn't have taken it, and, to be frank, I don't think Treena should have. But he has been such a pain to me over the years that I've known him, such a kvetch and a bore, I thought I deserved it, as compensation for all the crap I've listened to: No, the music press aren't conspiring against you. No, you don't look fat on TV. No, Dillon from Skyline isn't taken more seriously. Yes, you will make it past three albums. Yes, you will break America. Yes, I do like you for you and not because you're a celebrity.

Certainly by five, all the money was gone, although I'm not exactly sure what on. We went to a five-and-dime and blew loads of it on waterproof mascara, white nail varnish, vanilla-flavoured lip-balm, and bobby pins. We bought stationery pads printed with the Simpsons. We got tons and tons of candy that would melt before the day was out, never mind survive the plane trip home. I thought, as we sprinted from store to store, that it was a bonding experience. But when we spread out our purchases on the bed, I could tell that we were more excited about our haul than we were about each other.

I left Treena watching MTV with a rare-earth mud-mask on her face whilst I investigated the hotel. I was going through a really bad period of winking at people. I have no idea why. I winked at the bellboy, at the girls on reception, at the pretty gay boy delivering room service, at the cabdriver, at other guests.

I took the elevator up to the gym, which was on the seventh floor, at the end of the corridor behind a locked door that could be opened only with a big brass key. Such a buildup, my heart was thumping and I was expecting *Flowers in the Attic*. But behind the door, it was your standard gym, with a treadmill and several bikes and weight machines. I stood by the water dispenser and watched for a while as various hard-bodies pumped and pressed and preened. There was no one I recognised, so I continued on my wander.

I sat by the piano in the lounge and had a milkshake. I had to fight very hard against the urge to play "Heart and Soul." That's all I can play. I looked at the piano and saw myself, in my head, playing "Rhapsody in Blue." A genius of the ivories was studying me from behind an antique lamp. Doctor John or Dudley Moore, I couldn't decide. Okay, neither. It's my fantasy, why should there be an acknowledged piano player? I saw myself playing "Rhapsody in Blue" and it turned out Elizabeth Taylor was there and an excellent piano player.

She watched me for a while and was eventually so impressed by my skill that she couldn't help sliding onto the seat beside me and joining in. Then we played "Boys of Summer," which I'm not even sure has a piano in it. Nevertheless, we played it and when Elizabeth opened her mouth to sing, she had this big, fat blues singer's voice. It didn't suit the song, but I didn't stop her and she never missed a note. When we finished, she turned to me, clutched my hand, and, with a tear running down one cheek, stammered: "Richard never let me sing. He was worried I'd be better at it than him."

I met Treena and Ray at the pool at seven. He was in a surprisingly good mood and insisted that we go look in the Rocky and Bullwinkle shop across the road. This is a shop that sells nothing but Rocky and Bullwinkle merchandise: T-shirts, swimsuits, stickers, badges, socks. The plaster statues of the animated beaver and moose that sit astride the store are so huge, they cast shadows across the Chateau.

As soon as we walked through the door, I saw a china coffee mug and alarm clock with antlers that I had to have. Ray suggested I come back for it at the end of the week, which annoyed me. It was his idea to go in there and I am very bad at waiting for the right time to buy something. I prefer to buy it three days before a sale when it's full price, rather than three days later for half the cost. I enjoy it more. So what that my mug and clock would be sitting in the room until we went home? I wanted them and I made a face like a pound puppy until Ray relented and handed over the cash. Treena bought nothing.

That night Treena was gone again. I didn't notice until I woke, with a start, at 4:36. Four thirty-six in the morning is the scariest time alive. No one should be awake at 4:36. I listened for her in the pool, but all I could hear was a vague shuffle and groan that I didn't like at all. This time I felt very frightened and convinced myself that Treena had been a ghost all along, all the time I had known her. She had tricked me. Ghosts are clever. And they are attracted to teenage girls. Goddamnit, I had wasted an air ticket on a ghost. I wanted Manny. I wanted to climb in bed with him. But he was in London, so I put on my sandals and my courage and went to get Ray.

Between our bungalow and his lay a rockery. I stubbed my big toe on a rock, which, at that exact moment in time, I believed to be part of a human skull. My heart was pounding and I grabbed his door handle like a life raft and barged straight into his room without knocking. I heard heavy breathing and I thought it was my own, but it wasn't. I watched from the corner as Ray had sex with Treena. It was disgusting. She was facing the TV and he was ramming his groin against her buttocks. She was on all fours and her breasts hung down like on a statue of a mother wolf tending to her cubs. They were making horrible noises. He was calling her a bitch: "Jesus, you fucking bitch. You whore." She was screaming: "Come on, you cunt, you cocksucker. Fuck me harder."

I was so revolted by the act, by the words and the sounds, that I wasn't really bothered by the incidentals, such as: that was Treena and Ray, my two best friends, behind my back, fucking each other and fucking me over. I slipped out without making a noise and went back to my room. I was no longer scared. I opened the minibar and took out a bottle of cranberry juice and an almond Hershey bar. I ate it quite calmly and then rang Ray's room. He answered it with a groan.

"Ray, are you and Treena having an affair?"

"Oh my God."

I could hear her breathing hard. "What? Why have you stopped?"

"Ray, if you and Treena are having an affair, I don't mind."

"You don't?"

"No. I don't care." Which was not the truth in any way, shape, or form.

A tear skated towards my upper lip. "Ray, is Treena the girl from the Met Bar?"

He didn't answer and I hung up softly, flicked on the TV, and watched half an hour of the evangelist channel. I thought of Drew and how he hated sex. I missed him so much it was excruciating. I missed the glimpse I'd been given. Mostly I missed what I would never know, the talks we'd never have, the movies we'd never see, the friendship we'd never enjoy. I hated him for giving me a flake of his life, which is worse than nothing at all. I never had a chance to overeat, to make myself sick and swear I would never touch him again. I saw his brown skin shining in the sun, him walking real slow and smiling at everyone. What? I was delirious. He didn't have brown skin. It was white as pigeon shit. He never smiled. That's why I liked him. It was all too much.

I covered myself with blankets and sobbed. I made sure everything was hidden, from my toes to my hair. Why do people have to be so animal? Why do men want to fill women with a great, ugly, ungainly lump of themselves? Why do women want to be filled by men? How can they bear to bend over and contort their bodies to accommodate something so hideous? Why can't men and women just stroke each other's faces and keep their pants on? I lay rigid and cried, so I could feel everything and not lose a tear in the crevice of an elbow or a knee or a clump of hair.

Treena came creeping back in around dawn. She checked to see that I was asleep and eased herself under the covers.

"I'm awake."

I heard her softly start to cry: "I'm so sorry. I'm so sorry."

I felt terrible. She was in love. That's why she'd started working in school and lost her looks and become boring. It changes you. I, of all people, know how it feels. "It's okay." I got out of bed and put my arm around her.

"It is?"

"Yes."

She opened her green eyes wide and said, "Cool!" like she was in a 7 UP advert, and then she closed them again and fell fast asleep.

Ray was understandably edgy over breakfast. All he ate was some sliced grapes, but he swallowed each one with a gulp and a bulge of his eyeballs, as if he were actually eating syringes with spiders in them. I had a Chateau Marmont French Toast, which was divine. He didn't look at Treena, and I thought, "I'll be fucking furious if you finish with her, after all this, on the third day of bringing her over." Old Treena could have hitched her way around the country and got an airfare home without taking off her clothes, but spinach Treena was inevitably going to get fucked over by men. She'd take her clothes off and wouldn't ever see the money. As soon as she excused herself to go to the toilet, I told him that.

I said, "I forgive you, but now you've started, don't you dare give up. She's still my best friend. Don't break her heart. That would be embarrassing for all of us. That would make me hate you."

I was angry, but I was also intrigued to see how he acted with women he felt romantic towards. I had seen him chat up a girl only a couple of times and he had always been extremely drunk and useless. I wanted to see them holding hands, sharing cappuccinos, and whispering into each other's ears at concerts. I asked him how long he had felt this way about Treena, and he told me from the first moment he saw her. I thought back to when that was. It was a year ago, in my kitchen. He had come to return the video of *My Favorite Year* that he had borrowed from Manny. Treena and I had been up all night eating toffee popcorn and drinking Archers and orange. She had thrown up around dawn, and was now on the counter, wearing a long turquoise T-shirt, sipping Yop and trying to pull the congealed vomit out of her hair. She didn't acknowledge his presence. It was love at first sight.

I didn't laugh at him. I tried, but I couldn't do it. He's a phoney and he has a lot of faults, but in that instance he was not being treacly or untruthful.

"So do stuff together. Don't mind me. Be a couple."

"Oh, for God's sake, Viva. You're my two favourite girls. I want it to be all of us together."

"No you don't. Don't lie. You want me to sit on the end of the bed whilst you fuck? Okay, Captain Dostoevsky, tell me this. What do you talk about, when you're not having surreptitious sex, that is? Does Treena like to talk about Woody Allen with you? Because she doesn't to me."

He hung his head.

"And tell me one more thing. When you asked me to come here with you, what would have happened if I hadn't wanted to invite Treena? If I had asked to bring Manny instead? Would you have slept with him?"

Tears welled in his eyes and I let it go. Because he could not take it. We two ultra-strong people had sapped each other. Instead of combining their strength, they brought out these terrible characteristics in each other, traits from which they were previously immune. Treena had become boring and subservient, and Ray had become happy-go-lucky.

That night I told her it was okay if she wanted to go to Ray's bed, which she did. I ordered a typewriter to the room and wrote a really bad poem about Drew. I knew, as I was typing the words, that it was bad. I rifled through the fridge. Everything in it cost about five dollars. It was all being charged back to Ray, so I opened everything and licked it, then put it back. It was 11 P.M.

I rummaged through my wardrobe, but felt too lacklustre to dress up as anyone special. I put on my one pair of jeans, sneakers, and a T-shirt and went outside the hallowed doors of the hotel, out into the real world. The real world is no good, I thought, and stood rooted to the spot for a couple of minutes. People stared as they walked past me, in and out of reception, swinging delicate evening bags and smoking cigars. I looked left and right. Left was some road and right was some more road. I went right and found myself, after a few minutes, at the Comedy Store. After a little hassle with the doorman over my age, I paid to get in and saw Richard Pryor do a spot. He was shaky but absolutely brilliant. It was too smoky. I didn't feel scared. Part of that has left me forever and it makes me very sad. Now I think, if someone wants to shoot me and kill me, they can, so long as I don't see it happening.

I felt itchy and restless when I got back, so I had a cranberry and vodka and a Valium. It did the trick and I sunk into sleep. It pulled me down like quicksand. I held my breath and let go. The next day I felt like shit.

When I met them for breakfast, Ray and Treena had already been to the gym.

Treena was all excited, for the first time in forever. "I saw Leonardo DiCaprio."

I rolled my eyes. "I'll get the medal ready."

They were trying to be nice because they knew what they had done was shitty, and I was trying to be nice because I knew that Ray had paid for everything. They were better at it than me, which I found extremely insulting, considering they were clearly worse people.

I went out by the pool and waited until no one was looking and then pulled off my dress and jumped in the water. I was wearing a white one-piece with a keyhole cut beneath the bust, exactly like Liz in *Suddenly, Last Summer*. I knew it looked really good and, frankly, I was a bit embarrassed. When I pulled myself over the side, I saw that Dillon from Skyline was lying on a chair watching me. I adjusted my swimsuit and he waved me over.

"You're Ray's friend, aren't you?" He had a whiney voice for such a good singer.

"Yes. But not like that. God, no."

I slicked my hair back from my eyes. He grinned and clicked his fingers. "You look like Elizabeth Taylor in *Suddenly, Last Summer*."

"I do."

I meant to say "I do?" but I was so shocked that he could tell who I was dressed as that it came out all wrong. Like when you mean to say "Hello, how are you?" and it comes out "Hello, I hate you." I was standing over him and he had one hand over his eyes. Attack of the fifty-foot swimsuit.

"So, Dillon, what have you been up to?"

"I saw Leonardo DiCaprio having breakfast. I was going to twat the cunt."

"My best girlfriend is having an affair with my best boyfriend."

"Oh." He clicked his fingers again. "You win."

I felt really stupid, standing there having a conversation with a guy in an anorak whilst I was wearing a white swimsuit rendered see-through by the water. And I was dripping on his sneakers. I tried to think of some way to get away. "Where's your girlfriend?"

He cocked an eyebrow. "Which one?"

"The one from Brighton who was on the cover of Italian *Vogue*."

"Brighton, Brighton, Brighton . . ." he repeated, as if it were the chorus in a techno anthem. "Oh, she's not my girlfriend. Rather, I have a girlfriend and it is not she. Nah, she's just a bird I know. Do you wanna grab a chair?"

Not especially. But, let's face it, I didn't have anyone else to talk to. No one had tried to be my sugar daddy or put me in their film yet. So I sat down and attempted to arrange myself

NAMEDROPPER

so my thighs looked good, but whichever way I put them, they looked like they were about to take over the world. So I pushed the seat into a reclining position, lay down next to him, and pulled a towel over the whole of me, right up to my neck. His anorak was zipped up to the top, even though it was at least eighty-five degrees. I hoped he was topless underneath. He had on long shorts, which made him look double funny.

He fiddled with the zip. "I was just going to order from the menu. Do you want to have a look?"

I peered at it cautiously. Salads of baby tomatoes. Steamed vegetables. Fruit purée. Extra-creamy carrot cake. Oh, fuck it, I thought, I don't fancy him. I'll have what I want. "I like carrot cake."

"So do I."

"And chocolate cake."

"Cool." He beamed. "Let's have 'em both."

To be polite, I asked him about his various girlfriends, which, when I thought about it later, was not really very polite at all. He didn't care.

"I bet your friend from Italian *Vogue* doesn't eat chocolate cake."

"Nah, she doesn't. Boring bitch. But my proper girlfriend does. Tons of it. Eats it every minute of the day."

I was intrigued by his notion of "proper" and "not proper" girlfriends, like the latter category all had green slime instead of blood.

"I've been with my real girlfriend for five years. She's great. I completely dig her and respect her and want to spend the rest of my life with her. But I can't say I've ever been in love at any point in my life."

I wondered why he was telling me this and could only assume he must be very drunk. He kept wiping his nose with his sleeve.

"You sleep around, I take it?" I made it sound like "You have sugar with your tea, I take it?" He responded appropriately.

"Oh yes. Definitely. All the time."

What a freak. I wanted to get up and leave, but I found him quite compelling. Here was a pop star in excelsis. Telling a complete stranger his life story, as if everyone cared, not just his manager, accountant, drummer, and lawyer. Although I could see how he got confused. As we waited for our cake, Dillon told me that his girlfriend was a nursery school teacher and the first girl he'd ever kissed. They didn't live together—she still lived with her mother, to whom he felt very close. She hardly ever bothered to watch Skyline play because it wasn't her kind of music. He swore he would stop fooling around the minute he married her and that he would marry her in a flash if she would only agree.

"You see? I get infatuated with people and then I feel guilty. She doesn't know. I'll never leave her, but I have to be with other women. It makes our relationship stronger. I'm weak." He smiled, as if it were something to be proud of.

How very Victorian. One kind of sex that you have with fans and models, and one kind that you have with your girl-friend. What a sickening idea. By the time my two cakes arrived, I could barely swallow a mouthful.

"Eat up," he said, motioning to the cake. "I'm disappointed in you."

I squinted at him. "How can you be disappointed in me? If you don't know me, how can you expect anything of me? We only just met."

He shrugged his shoulders. "I'm easily disappointed."

"So am I," I said, starting to like him a little more than I had planned to, and suddenly determined to eat as much cake as I could. "So, let me get this straight. You get to sleep with hundreds of beautiful women and then you say, 'Hey, babe, sorry, but I can't give you my number because I've got a girlfriend who I love and adore.' Jesus. How cunning. And how much I admire you for it."

He started to laugh, a big booming, forgiving laugh. And I looked at him, in his zipped-up anorak and knee-length shorts, with his multitude of flings and his faithful long-term girlfriend, and I started to giggle uncontrollably. Our laughs mingled like a Mamas and Papas harmony. As we were hitting a high note, Ray came clomping along with his Ray-Bans perched on his nose. I was shocked at how American he looked.

He looked at us curiously, then turned away from me and said, "All right, Dillon? I'm staying in John Belushi's room."

"No you're not," I barked. "You're staying next door to where John Belushi died. Tell the truth. Next you'll be saying you are John Belushi." In light of recent events, I felt it my duty to become the guardian of justice. Dillon and I started laughing again.

That night Ray had a dinner with his U.S. press officer and Treena and I were forced to spend more quality time together.

I wanted to ask her sex questions: What was it like? What was he like? Didn't she find the hair on his neck a turnoff? How big was it? How did it happen? Was she in love? But I didn't. I asked her what she thought of the lipstick I had on, and she asked me if I wanted a stick of chewing gum.

I pulled on a cardigan and, in homage to Dillon, did it up to the top. We walked silently to the gigantic Virgin Megastore ten minutes up the road. It was so big it even housed a five-screen cinema. I wanted to see a film, but Treena said she was too jet-lagged to sit through anything. But not too jet-lagged to have animal sex all night. I bit my tongue. I really did and blood trickled down my chin. We went to the restroom and I stuffed my mouth with tissue. I knew she was ashamed to be seen with me. I wanted to stick a note in her mouth that read: "Really, she deserves to be seen with me because she stole my best friend." We bought a couple of CDs for the player in the room. Me: Cat Stevens, Kris Kristofferson, the soundtrack to *On the Town*. She: Toni Braxton.

"Be sure to play that to Ray when we get back. He loves Toni Braxton."

Treena turned her full attention on me for the first time in forever. "Does he?" She beamed hopefully.

I very slowly placed my hand on her shoulder and fixed her with my worst Nurse Ratchett face. "No."

I bought seven videos, even though I knew I wouldn't be able to watch them on my tape recorder at home. I liked the boxes. I like American lighting. It's always much too bright. Such forced hope. By the time I finished picking out my films, Treena was standing sullenly in the magazine section and my tummy was rumbling like an earthquake in a disaster movie.

We asked the twelve-year-old boy on checkout if he knew of a good restaurant nearby, thinking we could use Ray's credit card to get fancy. He directed us to Carney's, an enormous trailer with a café inside. I should have known from the name that it wasn't going to be contemporary French cuisine or raw fish. Thank God. Instead, we got enormous platefuls of chili, cheeseburgers, wet fries, and chocolate shakes in tall glasses. The food was brilliant. I kept nudging Treena and murmuring, "Isn't this incredible?" She nodded halfheartedly.

People have a hard time accepting that the best is the best, no matter what it's at: whether it's the best spit bubble, the best burp, the best graffiti, or the best handstand. If I had done a handstand in my History exam instead of just sitting there, I hope the adjudicator would have had the class to say: "Viva, you're clearly failing in History, but that is the best handstand I've ever seen." The best cheeseburger and fries is every bit as worthy as the best grilled swordfish.

I was furious with Treena for not getting more worked up about it. I didn't care about her sleeping with Ray, I just wanted her to chomp a french fry between her big white teeth and squeal, "Um, good!" I bet she'd do it for him. If she thought it would turn him on. I looked at her arms. He liked her because her body was entirely hairless. For the rest of the meal I tried to look at her face, but I could not drag my eyes away from her freakishly hairless arms.

We went back to the hotel and met up with Ray in the bar. He was perched on a high stool with some record executives and American management minions. He introduced Treena as his girlfriend. Wow. I excused myself to powder my nose, thinking about dusting it with gunpowder and then blowing them all up. On my way through the dimly lit bar, I passed Dillon. He had replaced the three-quarter-length shorts with a pair of skateboarder's trousers. But he still had on the anorak. It was still zipped up to the top. It actually seemed to be zipped further than the top, running on a track of its own. He was chatting up some six-foot amazon with a Dolce & Gabbana catsuit and dyed red hair. The highness of his top was matched by the lowness of her neckline, which almost reached her navel. When he spotted me, he quite literally pushed her to one side and sprinted to grab my arm. As the girl dusted herself down, he clung to my sleeve. He was so drunk that his right eye was twitching.

"Go back to your lady friend, Dillon. Don't even bother talking to me because—hey—I'm not going to sleep with you."

"That's what you think." He reeked of vodka, which isn't even supposed to smell of anything.

He gripped me tighter and whispered in my ear, "Take your clothes off."

I leaped away from him. "*What?*"

He said it louder. "Take your clothes off."

"What, here in the middle of the bar? No, I don't think so somehow."

He took this very well, backing off and nodding his head. "Okay, you're absolutely right." He rearranged his hair. "Take your knickers off."

For the second time that day, Dillon from Skyline made me double over with laughter. "Stop it. Oh, please stop it." I was laughing so hard tears were running down my cheeks and I had to grip his anorak for support. He readily held me up, with his hands around my waist.

"What's so funny, baby doll?"

"Oh, don't baby-doll me. Don't try and get off with me. You're embarrassing yourself. I don't like to see a man of your talent embarrassed like that." He chose to ignore me and tried to force his tongue into my mouth.

"Dillon, please stop it. You're just doing this to be polite, because I'm a girl and you're a big pop star and you think I'd be insulted if you didn't try and get off with me. You're not doing it because you fancy me. And that's more insulting for a girl like me."

He breathed a flame of vodka in my face and wailed, "I do fancy you."

Ray dragged himself away from Treena and the executives ("Treena and the Executives"—what a great name for a band). "Uh, what's going on?"

"Nothing, mate. Nothing. We were just talking about getting another drink." He put on an upper-class twit voice. "Join us, Raymond, in a glass of champagne. It's on me."

Nervously, Ray agreed, beckoning Treena over. The Dolce & Gabbana girl tried to sit down at our booth, but Dillon shooed her away, like she was a kitten with fleas, not an L.A. über-babe. We drank a magnum of champagne and then another one. Dillon and Ray went to the toilets together and, for five minutes, Treena and I were alone. I held her hand.

"Are you happy?"

"Yes." She smiled a hard, tight smile. I couldn't see her teeth.

"Good. So long as you're happy, then it isn't all in vain."

She looked over my shoulder into the middle distance, like I was a crazy lady. I let go of her hand. When they came back, Dillon and Ray seemed to be getting on like a house on fire. They had their arms around each other and kept singing bursts from each other's hits. Dillon even kissed Ray's forehead. They arm-wrestled for a bit, and then Dillon tried to play footsie with me under the table, but I kicked his foot away a bit too viciously and he cried out. Treena and Ray, who had been making gooey faces at each other, turned to stare, but Dillon just called the cocktail waitress over and started flirting with her and trying to look down her top. All of a sudden, I wanted him to look down my top. I wished I had kicked him a little more playfully.

When the bar closed, Dillon insisted that we all go back to his room to empty the minibar. He was booked into a suite on the top floor. We had to admit that it was even more impressive than our bungalows. It had a huge front room with a balcony, green velvet curtains, and views over the swimming pool. There were two desks, two brass hook telephones, and two luxuriously upholstered sofas. The kitchen had a cooker, a sink, and a tumble-drier. There were two bedrooms with two tall oak closets. This was all for Dillon, in case he got bored by one bedroom and had to get up and change in the middle of the night.

"Why aren't there two kitchens?" I asked, but no one was listening to me.

They were drinking red wine and tequila and snorting coke. I think the lovebirds were snorting tequila because, eventually, Ray passed out cold and Treena lay motionless on the floor. Dillon kept snorting away at his white powder. I didn't have any. I don't like things that look so pure when they're really so evil. If I wanted that, I'd just go out and snort Mia Farrow.

I stared out of the kitchen window, down onto the fifty-foot Marlboro Man sign. Music was blaring in the front room. I was sure we were going to get kicked out by management, so I sat, cross-legged, on the tumble-drier and admired the view before we got in trouble. I reached out a leg and flipped open the fridge with my foot, then bent down and grabbed a Coke. A piece of perfect gymnastics, and no one had seen it. I cocked my head. The Marlboro Man looks like Tom Selleck.

I must have been there for ten minutes when the music abruptly stopped and Dillon came stumbling into the kitchen. His anorak was finally unzipped. He had a white polo-neck T-shirt underneath. I was going to ask him how he could stand to dress like that in this heat, but instead I snapped, "Why are you called Dillon?"

He jumped back, bleary-eyed. "Well, uh, it's not my real name. My real name's Patrick. But I don't like it. Too Irishy-peasanty. I changed it to Dillon because of, well, you know . . ." He looked at his shoes.

"Because of Bob Dylan?"

"Yes." He ruffled his hair, which was starting to form kiss curls.

I put my hand clumsily on his shoulder. "I think that's lovely. Hey, I would change my name to Elizabeth Spring-steen if I had the nerve. But why don't your songs sound like Bob Dylan?"

"Don't they?" He looked devastated.

"Um, not really. You sound Beatlesy and Stonesy, even Who-y. But not Dylany. Sorry. Hey, do you want to hear me sing 'Leopard-Skin Pill-box Hat'?"

He clapped politely.

He told me that Dylan was his big love, that he had intended to be a folk singer, but all his mates had laughed at him. The way he told it, it was less that he succumbed to some Valley Girl notion of peer pressure than that he felt he had a duty by his friends. If they wanted him to play football and be in their band, he would.

"They must have known what was best for me because it paid off, didn't it?" He walked in a tiny circle, as big as a cheddar-cheese cracker. "I just play the music, sing what they want. They don't like folk. They don't even like Bob anymore. Someone like Ray can get away with talking about being inspired by this mad fucker or that mad fucker, but not me. I'm just some daft scouse chancer."

I could still taste the Carney's burger in the back of my throat. "If that's what they think, then you be the best daft scouse chancer you can. Don't be like Ray. You don't have to tell the world's media about your favourite films. Ray goes on and fucking on about Woody Allen and I don't think anyone believes him. Keep Bob for yourself. It makes it more special. Why waste your breath on those bozos?" I paused. "I'm hungry."

We toasted S'mores, which are the purest form of junk food there is, in that they take some skill to make. This entails holding marshmallows over the stove until they dribble, but not until they burn, and then placing them between a slab of Hershey's chocolate and a Graham cracker. I made them silently, thinking, "I hope he doesn't think I'm acting like a wife," and "If I ever do become a wife, I hope I never have to make anything but S'mores." Dillon stuffed the canapé in his mouth and pink marshmallow crept down his chin. I asked him if he was going to be sick, and he said he wasn't planning on it.

"You're a good kid. I like you. I either hate people, don't notice them, or get obsessed by them. I never just plain like someone." He swallowed the last mouthful of goo. "Who are you obsessed by?"

I pushed myself back onto the tumble-drier and took a deep breath. "Drew. He had that band, The Kindness of Strangers."

Dillon licked his fingers. "Never 'eard of them."

"No, they weren't really famous. They weren't even very good. But he had something." I reconsidered this. "He had everything."

Dillon took his anorak off and hung it on the chair. "Do you want to crash here?"

I was three minutes from my own bed. It wasn't like I was stranded in Tottenham and I couldn't get a cab home. But I thought about the question and concluded that I did want to stay.

"I can sleep in the spare bedroom."

"Nah." He didn't explain why. He just calmly dismissed the notion.

"Well, we can at least move Ray and Treena."

"They can stay on the floor like the dogs they are."

The minute we got back in the bedroom he became very

polite. The TV was flickering with the sound on low. He snorted the last of the coke.

"Do you mind if I take off my shoes?" I told him I'd mind more if he kept them on. I asked if I could borrow a T-shirt, and he turned away whilst I wriggled out of my shirt and pulled it over my head. Then he turned off the lights and whipped his T-shirt off so he was wearing only his boxer shorts. He leaped under the covers so fast he scratched my arm with his fingernail.

"What's the matter with you?"

"I don't like my body. Too skinny. Like Bob."

"But you have a lovely body," I lied. It *was* kind of disgusting, so pale and chickeny. I don't know why I felt the need to boost the ego of a Lothario who regularly cheated on his girlfriend of five years.

We lay flat on our backs for a few minutes, a foot apart. Then he reached out and held my hand. He wasn't turned towards me, so we must have looked like we'd been arranged in a strange burial position. He stroked my fingers and turned them over in his hand, gently brushing each fingernail.

"What scent are you wearing?"

I thought it was really cool that he said "scent" and not "perfume," and I wouldn't have liked him so much if he hadn't. He leaned over and breathed against my neck. He was supposed to be smelling *me*, but all I could feel was him blowing *out*. He put his tongue in my ear, which sounds like something disgusting from a ZZ Top video, but was actually really nice. He put one hand around the back of my neck and slipped the other under the curve of my back, and pulled me tight to him. I felt embarrassed because my breasts were squashed against him, but then I opened my eyes and he didn't look like he minded too much.

Then he bit my neck and started licking my chin. He pulled himself on top of me and moved downwards, kissing my tummy.

"Tell me what you like."

"I like cola-bottle sweets. I still like leggings under mini-skirts, even though Madonna hasn't worn them in ten years. I like Bruce Springsteen and Hello Kitty. I like movies made before 1967. What do you like?" He lifted his face from my stomach and I wished I hadn't asked.

"I like Bob Dylan and girls in patent-leather T-bar shoes, smart shoes, not sneakers. I like nail polish and round faces. I like Marmite on toast. My favourite album is *Blood on the Tracks*." He giggled. "These are a few of my favourite things."

"Well, look, to be honest, every musician likes Bob Dylan. Who doesn't like Bob Dylan? That doesn't count."

"Okay, I like John Denver."

"That's better." I stroked his face and he kissed me very softly.

"I like that. I like kissing."

We went to sleep for a few hours. Every so often I would stir and he would kiss my neck. I woke up and he was staring at me.

"I do fancy you. You said I was just trying to get off with you because you were there. Don't think that."

"Great, fine, whatever. Let me go to sleep."

Around noon, I woke up with my nose in Dillon's armpit. I delicately rearranged myself and sat up to watch MTV. When

Ray came to, he talked to me quite normally for about three minutes, until I rearranged the covers around me and he said, in a strangulated yelp, "Oh my God. You're wearing your pants." I replied that of course I was wearing my pants, that they were big pants, and that I also had a bra on. The bra was, admittedly, quite small and seemed to have shrunk in the night. Possibly Dillon had chopped it up and snorted it when I wasn't looking.

FOURTEEN

I was going to say, "Dillon, I'm in love with you," which was the truth at the time, whilst he was kissing my tummy and telling me how beautiful I was. Treena would have killed me if I had, but I was kind of sorry I didn't because, soon, the moment had passed and though we clearly liked each other a lot, we weren't in love anymore and never would be again. If I said it, would we have been able to make it last longer? Or would I have had to leave the room then and there?

When we finally slapped Treena awake, gathered up our shoes, and left, Dillon was conked out and snoring. The next time I saw him was at four-thirty that afternoon, as I surfaced for air in the swimming pool. Chlorine stung my eyes, and I saw the glare of his anorak before I saw him.

He sat on the edge of the deep end and dangled his legs in the water. "Your nose is burning," he called.

"Your anorak is unzipped," I called back.

Then I swam towards him, stopped two feet away, and began to tread water. "You don't have to talk to me again. I know the routine."

He ushered me closer with a wave of his hands, as if I were a plane coming in to land. "I *want* to talk to you again."

"Okay," I fluted, "talk to me, because I'm leaving tomorrow."

He nodded his head bravely. "Are you going to go back to England with them?"

"Yep. Got my seat booked and everything."

He nodded some more and fiddled with his zip. "Um. I'm going to Las Vegas tomorrow. We've got a showcase Saturday night at the Hard Rock Café Hotel."

"That's nice."

"Yeah, it is." He zipped and unzipped. "Why don't you come with me?"

I held my breath, ducked down to the bottom, and did a handstand. That was my deal with myself: if I can do a handstand underwater, I'll go with him. He didn't know that, and was peering anxiously at the bubbles when I surfaced. "Okay, I guess."

If anyone ever asks me to marry him, I'll do a handstand, and if I don't fall, I'll land on my feet and say, "Okay, I guess." I didn't worry about money or booking a flight or how I would eventually get home, or if Manny would mind.

Ray was not at all happy about it. He said a flat no, until I reminded him that any notion he might have had of being a father figure was most likely negated by his sexual relationship with my best friend. Treena, to her credit, argued my cause with passion. She turned out not to be an irredeemably bad person. "This is a once-in-a-lifetime chance for her."

Ray thought that staying at the Chateau Marmont was a once-in-a-lifetime chance.

"For you and me, maybe. Not for Viva. She'll probably be

living here in five years' time. Whatever she does, she will live an elegant life. But she hates vulgarity. And in five years my Viva will be too embarrassed to have a dirty weekend in Vegas. That is something she can only do either before she turns twenty or after she hits seventy. I've been waiting, since I met her, for her to act like a teenager. You even said it yourself. So here it is. You have to let her go."

"It's not a dirty weekend," I stammered. In the end, Ray didn't so much give me his blessing as wash his hands of me.

Treena helped me pack, sat on my suitcase for me as I attempted to close it. No matter how I tried, I couldn't fit in the Rocky and Bullwinkle alarm clock. I gave it to her. If she didn't want it, she could leave it for the room. We shared the last of a bag of pretzels and a can of Coke and curled up together on the bed. She was not the same. Not even her body, increasingly slender and hard, felt the same. But the action was familiar—we had fallen asleep like that so many times before—and that gave me some comfort.

Soon she was asleep and whistling through her nose. I extricated myself from her hairless arms and went to return my typewriter to reception. I asked the night man if Antonio Banderas had rung for me. He didn't miss a beat. "I'll just check." No, Mr. Banderas had not rung. Not yet.

The air was balmy and I wandered through the back entrance of the hotel out onto the street. I wanted to take a photo of the Rocky and Bullwinkle shop. I was skirting left and right, trying to find the best angle, when I heard a woman call "Hello." I walked a little way down the slope and saw a Hispanic girl sitting on the steps of a Psychic Help shop. There are hundreds of Psychic Help shops in L.A., most of them makeshift shacks. They form a sort of shanty town of hope against logic. I've laughed at them a hundred times, imagined what kind of saddo goes in there and lays down cash they don't have, to be told they will attract a lot of money in the future. Unhappy people, who have never recovered from not being discovered by Steven Spielberg. Thirty-five-year-old men too old to play the ingénue, too young to spend the rest of their lives being waiters, old enough to know that that's what will happen anyway.

"Hello. You want me to read your palm? I'm getting very impressive psychic vibes off you. I could feel them from all the way down the street." This girl was my age and beautiful, apart from her incredibly buck teeth. "It's only five dollars."

"Only five dollars."

"Yes." Her voice was so serene and her hair was so pretty. She had told me I had impressive psychic vibes. She had complimented me. If someone told me I had impressive boogers, I would want to be their friend. She took my five dollars and sat me down under a purple lampshade. When she took my hand, it sent an uncomfortable twinge up my arm because I was seated too far away. I wanted to tell her, but I was worried about interfering with her reading. Her black brows furrowed.

"Someone is jealous of you. A woman with brown hair. Do you know who this could be?"

Thinking about it now, all women have brown hair. Hardly anyone is really a blonde. But I wanted the psychic to like me and I told her that I knew exactly who she was referring to.

"They have cast a dark spell on you. You have a wonderful, bright aura. But every day your aura is getting a shade blacker.

If this is not reversed, then eventually . . ." She caught her breath and so did I.

"For your own good, you must let me help you. I am going to light candles for you and I am going to pray for you."

"Thank you. Thank you so much."

She gripped my hand. "The prayer will cost ninety dollars and the candles will cost a hundred dollars."

Tears of humiliation stumbling down my face, I gave her everything I had. Thirty-two dollars and one quarter. She told me she expected to see the rest of it tomorrow.

I spent a sleepless night under the blankets, boiling hot, but terrified of uncovering any part of me. When I met Dillon in the lobby the next day, my skin was grey and my eyelids purple. I thought I'd better tell him what had happened in case he thought I was a smackie and decided not to take me to Vegas. He wanted to go round and bust up the shop and get my money back. But when we got there it was all boarded over. A couple of doors down from the boarded-up shop was a tattoo parlour. So instead of getting back my money, we went next door and got tattooed instead. If I had thought about it, I wouldn't have done it, but Dillon took my hand, sat me down, and said, "She'll have that." He picked out a heart with ivy around it. I was so angry that he had chosen on my behalf that I forgot I didn't want a tattoo at all.

"No, I'll have that." I pointed at a sketch of a violet. "To remind me of Elizabeth Taylor's eyes."

"Where do you want it?"

"On her bum," ordered Dillon.

"Not on my bum. On my tummy."

The tattooist was a massive skinhead. Why aren't there

beautiful tattooists? It would make the whole art seem far less intimidating.

He opened a clean needle in front of me and then leaned over and got to work. It felt like someone was pinching me very hard. If I hadn't been with someone I was trying to look pretty in front of, I think it would have hurt a lot worse. As it was, I let my body relax and tried to ride out the pain. I was glad I couldn't see. Dillon cried more than I did. He had settled on a detailed depiction of a tiger holding a banner that said FREEWHEELIN'. It took almost forty-five minutes. He already had one tattoo, of an iguana, on his back. But it was not very impressive. In fact it looked more like a stain or a piece of mould than a tattoo. They taped bandages to our wounds, took our money, and told us that a scab would form and then fall off after a week. Dillon paid for both of us and walked back to the hotel with his elbow at a right angle. He said it made him feel better.

"How are you going to sing?"

"I don't sing with my arm."

"I know, but you look so funny."

But within an hour the pain had subsided to the extent that I got up the courage to ring Manny and tell him I was not coming home as planned. We chatted for a bit, about the weather and seeing Natalie Portman. Then I told him not to get angry, but I had something to confess.

"Oh my God. Did you get tattoos?"

"That's a funny question. Um. I didn't get tattoos, plural."

He started to hyperventilate. Then he caught himself and started yelling. "You stupid, stupid girl. How could you muti-

late your body like that? You, a Jew, whose people were mutilated against their will." I would carry that thought with me
for the rest of my life. In that second, my violet lost its appeal.
I knew Elizabeth Taylor would not approve of it. The call was
costing about five dollars a minute. I racked my brains for
something to win him over, some brilliant argument that
would make it all right.

"But Manny, they look so pretty on Drew Barrymore."

He actually screamed. Like a girl. Like a girl getting a tattoo. "And you would do something just because Drew Barrymore did it?"

"Do you really want me to answer that? Because if you
really want me to answer, I will."

After all that, telling him I was going to Vegas with an inter-
national rock star I had only just met was pretty small potatoes.

The short plane ride was not the most comfortable experience
of my life, even though we were on the leather-upholstered pri-
vate jet owned by the head of Skyline's record label. I had to sit
bolt upright not to scratch my wound on my vest. Dillon still
had his arm stuck out at a right angle. The rest of the band had
flown out to Vegas the day before on a BA flight. Skyline
weren't playing for four days, but the label was so pleased
with them that they decided to show them a good time in the
city of sin. Everything was paid for in advance: the flights, the
suites, the room service, the limos, the money to go gambling, the money the band would lose gambling.

I was nervous that Dillon might run off and leave me the
moment he was reunited with his scally mates. But when we

met them in the lobby, he held my hand. He could have wrapped his arm around my waist, or placed it on my bottom. Or stood three feet away. So I was rather moved at this gesture of non-aggressive friendship. His peers were vaguely sketched versions of him with police lineup alterations: the drummer had a boss eye, the bass player had a beer belly, the guitarist had a broken nose. They were friendly, if slightly suspicious of me.

If the Chateau Marmont would be played by Angelica Huston, the Hard Rock Hotel and Casino would have to be played by Pamela Anderson. It's eye-catching and thrilling, but ultimately unenlightening and a little goes a long way. Our room was amazing, but it scared me a bit. It had a bathroom on both sides of the hall and a Jacuzzi in the middle of the lounge. I guess everyone who sets up in Vegas knows what a filthy town it is. The bed was about the size of Sweden, and over the seven fat pillows at the head hung a huge framed photo of Mick Jagger. Dillon launched into a very poor impression.

"Start me up! Well, if you start me up, I'll never stop!"

"That's what I'm worried about, mate."

We went and dumped our bags and headed straight down to the casino to start gambling on the Jimi Hendrix and Sex Pistols slot machines. There were German tourists and Hell's Angels and Mafiosos and Been There Babes, but mostly there were old people, anywhere and everywhere. And this is Las Vegas's premier rock 'n' roll hotel. I was prepared, because Tom Wolfe had described the town as "Disneyland for OAPs," but I think Dillon was a bit freaked out. Only ten dollars down and he suggested we go outside and sunbathe for a while.

The hotel swimming pool was a re-creation of a California beach, with palm trees, golden sands, and wave machines. It was accurate in every detail, other than that the California sea does not, to my knowledge, have Crosby, Stills, and Nash piped underwater twenty-four hours a day. Classic Rock was, as was to be expected, the name of the game. It just kept popping up in the most surprising places: even the elevator was swathed in leopard print and adorned with an Aerosmith quote. It did feel odd to be standing next to Dillon, in an elevator packed with white-haired ladies in pantsuits, under an enormous gold sign reading LOVE IN AN ELEVATOR—LIVIN' IT UP WHEN I'M GOIN' DOWN.

Even though that was what I wore when I first met him properly, I was embarrassed to be in my swimsuit in front of Dillon. So I did what I did the first time and covered myself with a towel. Neither of us could get wet because of the tattoos. We had nothing to do but spread out on loungers and drink margaritas. Dillon had to order them because they wouldn't serve me without proof that I was twenty-one. He ordered one for himself, many times over, and shared it with me when the waitress wasn't looking.

The cocktail eradicated the pain of the tattoo and thoughts of Treena, Ray, and Drew. I felt all remnants of Drew wash out of my body, as if someone were sucking them out through my little toe. Before long, the towel was on the floor and my arms were crossed behind my head. The tattoo itched, but the sun warmed my legs and face and I felt like a cat on a windowsill. And the sun was studded with rhinestones. Every now and then, Dillon would reach across from his recliner and lay a hand on my elbow. The music blared across the sun deck, a pleasant run of Fleetwood Mac, Beatles, and Tom Petty, blighted by occasional patches of Genesis or Whitney Houston.

Then the inevitable happened. The song I most and least hoped for every time I encountered a radio tuned to FM. The opening chord struck my cool like the cry of an Arizona bird of prey that got horribly lost and ended up with the seagulls, circling Brighton Pier. This wasn't the time or the place, with this person I didn't know, for such incandescent beauty. I blocked my ears but the words forced my fingers apart with kisses and promises that they'd always be there for me. I forced my head onto my shoulder, but I could still hear it.

". . . *those days are gone forever, I should just let them go but . . .*"

Dillon leaped up and kneeled beside me, blocking my sun. "Don't cry, Viva, please don't cry. What's wrong?"

". . . *after the boys of summer have gone . . .*"

I was so embarrassed, I had to pretend that I was abused as a child and that something had just triggered a bad memory. That it was that, and not a Don Henley song, that had made me break down. He all but carried me back to the room, where he drew the curtains and started running me a bath. I managed to mumble that I couldn't because of the tattoo, but he said that we were being overcautious, he'd done it before and it would be fine. I made him have one too and he did, but in the other bathroom. He filled both tubs with bubbles and opened the two connecting doors to the living room so that we could talk and see each other whilst we bathed.

I sank underwater and counted to ten. When I came up for air, he was calling, "Viva! Viva!"

I blew my nose on a hand towel. "What?"

"Tell me something about you that I don't know."

"Anything? But, honey, there's so much to tell!" Well, there was and there wasn't. There's so much to tell, unless you edit your memories without sentimentality or vanity. Absolutely everything looks significant if you remember it. In fact, you remember the least important bits. I can count to ten in French. I'd rather be able to talk about Truffaut in French and once upon a time, for about a day, I believed I could. The next day I forgot, and nothing could bring it back. That's when I realised French was a lost cause.

"Okay, here's something. I saw *Carrie* when I was eight. I didn't realise until four years later that I was scared. One day I woke up and just collapsed back in my bed and cried for a whole morning because I was so frightened."

He yelled back, "That's nothing. I slept in my parents' bed for a whole year after I saw *Evil Dead*."

"Euw. Now you tell me something else I don't know yet."

He told me that he thought Sissy Spacek had one of the most beautiful faces he'd ever seen and I made a mental note: not good.

"Everyone knows who your top beauty is." He started to caw in a high Southern accent: "I'm alive! Maggie the Cat is alive!"

"That's true. I love Elizabeth Taylor because she is a short girl with a weight problem who is torn between being highly sexual and wanting to settle down and get married. I feel a bond, but so what? You love Bob Dylan because he excuses your foibles."

"Do tell."

"It's obvious. He's a not very attractive man with a whiney voice who got incredible fame and fortune and slept with hundreds of beautiful women."

Dillon let his foot drop with a splash. "I'm not very good-looking, am I?"

I stroked my calf with a razor. "Your skin is very soft." When Manny is trying to be nice about someone and he can't think of anything else to say, he says they have nice handwriting.

We dried off, put fresh knickers on, and got in bed. I touched his cheek and he pulled me close and didn't let go for a long time. Then he kissed me. Afterwards I wiped my mouth.

"What did you do that for?"

"Boy germs."

We snuggled for a bit. I imagined I was a cat and prodded his chin with my head. Then I climbed on top of him and poked a finger into his chicken chest. "You haven't tried to have sex with me."

"I know. It's not that I don't find you attractive. I think you're gorgeous. But I don't feel like I want to jump on you and have rampant rumpy-pumpy." The sweating, pumping beast that was Treena and Ray flashed in front of my eyes. Dillon continued, "I just want to hold you and kiss you. I don't get a chance to do that very often. You don't mind, do you?"

I loved it. I loved that he hadn't tried to put his hand down my pants or any of the other terrible, embarrassing things that Treena had always warned me about. It was as if we didn't exist between the hips and the knees. Even though we spent every night that week with our legs wrapped around each other, the middle part was invisible, like in a science-fiction movie.

Earlier I had dragged him into Tower Records and made him buy *Darkness on the Edge of Town* by Bruce Springsteen. I padded over to the hi-fi and put it on. He said it made him think of his father and cried, and I secretly fantasised about what his father might look like with no shirt on. I pictured a short, stocky man with an overbite, curly, thinning hair, and biceps like Popeye. He cried quietly and, a little cruelly, I said, "See. Now do you get it? Bruce is the new Bob Dylan, not you, you daft bastard."

The next day we decided to dress up as Bob and Liz and imagine what kind of relationship they might have had. I felt two things: one, that I was five years old, tipping over the dress-up box; two, that I might have just found my soulmate. We planned it over breakfast. I was going to be *Suddenly, Last Summer*–era Liz and he was going to be "Don't Look Now" Bob. We wouldn't see each other until that night at dinner, like the groom can't look at the bride before the wedding. Dillon didn't have a whole lot of dressing up to do. Dark shades are easy-peasy to buy in Vegas.

But I had to find a medium-length black wig, a low-cut white dress tied ruthlessly at the waist, high white pumps, and a scarf for my hair, all of which I did. The difficult thing was the wig. I had to go by bus, way out into no-man's-land, and find a really tacky, out-of-date five-and-dime where they thought the nineties had not yet started. I knew it was a promising sign when I saw a big poster of Madonna in her "Get into the Groove" era getup. It was worth it. Dillon said I was the most beautiful girl he had ever seen. He had teased his hair into a Jewish Afro and had drainpipe trousers and wrap-around shades.

He looked stoopid, with two o's. Indeed, the mood was so deliriously stoopid that he persuaded me to take some of his coke. We spent our evening tearing around the casino, placing money on the black, the red, and the red, white, and blue for all we knew. There are no locks and no windows in Las Vegas casinos, so that you get disorientated and spend money for three days straight. We had no idea what time it was when we collapsed under Mick Jagger.

Here are some things Dillon said to me that night:

"When you close your eyes, you look like a vulnerable little girl, but when you open them, I feel like you can see through my soul."

"You have the most perfect lower back I've ever seen."

"You're dangerous: that body combined with that brain is very frightening."

"When I first saw you, I was so jealous of Ray for being with you. I hoped and prayed I'd bump into you again."

Here are some things he said during the day:

"Stop jumping on the bed, I feel sick from last night."

I managed to wake him at four and drag him to the nearest mall. We bought Simpsons' trading cards from a comic-book store and went to see a scary movie that was supposed to be post-modern and ironic, but that was really just scary. We thought there was a killer in front of us—he was the only one there apart from us, and kept breathing much too loud—but when the lights came up, we saw that he was mentally disabled. Taxi fares in and out of the Strip were ludicrous, at least twenty dollars a throw. I felt bad that Dillon was paying for it, but he didn't. He has this Liverpool thing about girls not having to pay. Feminism goes out the window when you find yourself in Vegas on a whim. Ray paid for things—he brought me to L.A., after all—but he always made such a big deal of it. Dillon let on that the first thing he had done when he made it was retire his parents, who are real Irish peasants, to a farmhouse.

He took cocaine all week long, in larger amounts the closer it came to Skyline's showcase gig. He didn't spend much time with the band—joining them, occasionally, for one drink at the bar, then making his excuses and trotting along the corridor after me. Still feeling lousy from the night before, we crept back to the room, but were stopped by two painted girls who wanted Dillon's autograph. They couldn't have been more than fourteen, but were wearing matching Lycra minidresses, scarlet lipstick, and garish blue eye shadow. He chatted pleasantly to them and they, as if I wasn't there at all, started asking if they could come back to his room. He said he was feeling tired. To my horror, the girls began to paw each other, caressing their tiny breasts with their bitten fingernails. "C'mon. We're only fifteen. You should look after us. You should teach us." They looked like a freak show. I started giggling and unlocked the door. Dillon brushed them away and followed me, latching the door behind him.

I tried to string a sentence together. All I could come up with was, "That was . . . weird."

Dillon turned on the TV and sniffed. "Not so weird. All female fans just want to be fucked until they bleed."

I slapped him so hard that he fell sideways. I had no idea where it had come from, but come it did, at ninety miles an hour. He was on all fours. I was so embarrassed that I had to lean out of the window.

"What was that about?"

"I don't know."

"I don't like that. I was slapped around as a child. And I don't like that."

"I'm sorry."

The next morning he said he had to go to the conference room and do an interview with *Spin* magazine. I tried to kiss him and blow in his ear but he didn't respond. So I showed how much I didn't care by pretending to write in my notebook. What I wrote was:

> This is it. He doesn't want to hug me anymore and I don't know what to do and he's gone forever and please let me be cool and let him go and act like a grownup, like I don't care just keep writing and he won't know my heart is breaking.

He started to get dressed and as I was telling myself "*Act cool*," I found I was clinging to his leg. He looked down and smiled like I was a disappointing child who had promised to put herself to bed and was up watching TV.

"Please give me a hug." He leaned down halfheartedly and pressed my sides like I was an easy-squeeze ketchup bottle, not a proper English one made out of glass. Then he pulled away and I grabbed his arm and beseeched him, "Please, Dillon. Tell me a story."

It was a very poor story, about a princess in a tower. I told him it was a silly story, but he said that was the best he could do, and continued dressing. I thought of Ray becoming bored with me in the car on the way to Brighton. I saw that Dillon had now had his fill too. And I hadn't even put out. Apart from dancing in my underwear, spitting out of windows, gambling, dressing as Elizabeth Taylor, getting a tattoo, and slapping him round the face. I had fit a five-year relationship into five days and now he wanted back his real five-year girlfriend, with whom he had done none of these things.

Drew had never once been bored by me. Partly because he disappeared from my life before Viva overkill could kick in and partly because he was never interested in the first place.

Dillon came back from the interview saying how great the journalist had been, how sexy she was. We slept in the same bed that night, but far apart. I watched him, tried to memorise his tattoos (one fresh and one mouldy), his every freckle and hair, all the while forgetting what his face looked like. I lifted the cover from the bottom end of the bed and looked at his feet. He had dancer's feet, with all the toes practically the same length. I smelled his hair. It reeked of cocoa butter and I saw that I had made him smell of me. He didn't have a smell of his own.

I kissed his forehead and wept the silent, self-loathing tears of a mother leaving her child for a new life. She knows no one will be as good to her little boy as she would. No one will love him as much. She knows that he will be looked after but that he will never again encounter anyone who understands him as well. Thank God, the little boy doesn't know that. Dillon from Skyline slept peacefully, dreaming of lipstick prints on tissue, chips in vinegar, patent-leather shoes, Sissy Spacek, waterbeds, and *Blood on the Tracks.*

I kissed him but I knew it was all finished and we hadn't even had a love affair. I didn't think we had, although I wasn't sure. He snored and I watched him for a while longer, kneeling in front of his face so he could only possibly be breathing in my breath. Then I called a cab and went to the airport. I cashed in all my traveller's cheques and managed to get a flight direct from Vegas to Heathrow. As I waited in departure, I noted that it was only ten hours until Skyline's big sold-out gig. They would go down a storm. He would meet a nice girl to spend the night with. I cried a lot on the plane. Because I was in economy, and nothing I said could get them to upgrade me. Because I knew now that it was Dillon and not Drew who was the love of my life and he had never even been my lover. Because we had had so much fun. And because I had never really especially liked him in the first place. Because it was he who liked me and pursued me and made me feel so much better about myself. And because things change. I wasn't sorry that I had the tattoo on my tummy. The lights were dimmed and I leaned my head against the shutter.

A little voice inside my head said, "Don't look back, you can never look back."

I realised that just because someone likes some of the same films as you, it doesn't mean you're going to live happily ever after. It was the films he liked that I liked, rather than he himself. It's overoptimistic to think that your soulmate marks himself out by having heard of your favourite movie. All men can be educated. Dillon just happened to have a head start. So he had seen *Suddenly, Last Summer*. It could have been anything. He was an empty vessel. It might have been football. Indeed, when he was with the rest of the band, or singing for the fans, he pretended it was. It could have been ballet that he knew about, or cheeses of the world, or Russian history. With these thoughts came the sneaking suspicion that I was a real live grownup. It wasn't as terrible and traumatic a feeling as I had imagined it might be.

I thought of him, with his feet in the Chateau Marmont pool and his fork in a carrot cake. He was just a little kid. I was upset at what I had introduced him to, the records and films he didn't already know. I felt like a mother who had left syringes around the room and let her baby get hooked on hard drugs.

I felt very worried that I had perhaps not been discriminate enough in my cultural sharing. I was too easy with him. I had been too eager to educate him about Elizabeth, giving away all my favourite films, books, and records. Really, it was as slutty as putting out on a first date. I hadn't made him work for it. That I had listened to *Darkness on the Edge of Town* with him and watched *Harold and Maude* wrapped up with him on his hotel bed. I was terrified that I might have somehow, through my actions, wiped them from my existence, the world over. I was too scared to listen to my Springsteen tape because I knew it would consist entirely of feedback and crackle. Kids would learn about Springsteen in history class and mystery would surround the alleged fourth album. The kids, without evidence to convince them, would not believe it had ever really existed, and in time the mere suggestion would be discredited entirely.

FIFTEEN

I don't know how I kept my mind free of Drew for so long, but
when I got home, Manny told me that the police had found
his body. I didn't cry. I didn't know him. Manny says he is glad
I went away, that I have matured. But I don't think so. I spent
the summer break being rather than seeing. I hate it. I don't
remember anything at all. I know what I did well enough to
write a "My Holidays" diary: went to Los Angeles with Ray
and Treena, realised they were having an affair, eloped to Las
Vegas with a rock star, yadda yadda yadda. But it's no good to
me. The details aren't there because I was . . . I was too busy to
make notes. They tricked me, Ray and Manny and Treena.
They made me think it was an experience I couldn't pass up,
a real big-budget film for me to star in. And it was all a ruse to
make me stop watching films for a few weeks, to make me
stop dreaming about Drew.

Things never come out the way you want them to, not if
you speak them out loud. The minute you let the words out of
your mouth, they react with the air and there's nothing you
can do to change them back. Francis Ford Coppola readily
admits that *Apocalypse Now* turned out very differently from
the vision in his head. Sure, everyone thinks it's one of the
greatest films of all time, but that doesn't change the fact that

it wasn't what he had intended it to be. I can't watch it because I'm obsessed with the other version, the one he couldn't communicate.

I failed the exams. Those I turned up for. Considering the amount of effort I made to fail, this did not surprise me. The school accepted that I was under mental strain and that the results were unreflective of my true ability. Manny said he was very disappointed. I said to him, "Manny, did you ever once see me revise?" He knew there was no way I could pass, yet he thought it would still come right. According to the rules, I should have done fabulously well because that's what would happen at the end of a film. The rebel comes right. I tried to reason with him: "It only happens because scriptwriters are too lazy to think of a proper ending. Like at the end of *Grease*, when John Travolta and Olivia Newton-John take off in a flying car. Hello?"

"It happens because people do their work. It happens because people have more pride than to waste their potential."

I thought about the flying car. "No, I really don't think that has a lot to do with it."

So I don't get to go to university. So I have to go out into the world right now and stake my claim.

Treena did work hard and, not illogically, it paid off. She passed everything and got a 96 percent in Religious Studies. I feel it is not a coincidence that Treena hates films. The part of her that can't sit still that long in the dark can sit still that long under the underpaid gaze of the adjudicator. Ray was immensely proud of her. "My girl's got brains." I thought it was a little sick to talk about it. It rubbed in the fact that she was three years old and he was a hundred. He took her to The Ivy to celebrate—she told me about it the next day. She said that there wasn't a lot she could eat because it all had green stuff sprinkled on top.

"Herbs?"

"Yes," she answered, eyes narrowing at the memory. "Them."

Treena was pretty much staying at Ray's every day of the week. Whenever I rang for him, she picked up the phone, and whenever he rang me, I could hear her burbling, "Say hi from me!" in the background. They planned to move in together officially once Treena was at college—which is nice if you want to see your two dearest friends at once and not so nice if you're thinking of a cunning plan to turn them against each other. I trusted they'd work that one out soon enough for themselves, without me having to waste my precious time.

I asked her if she had seen Marcus lately and she had to be reminded who he was.

Time seems all the more precious when you spend it by yourself. All the time with Treena was crammed full of friendship bracelets, M&M's, face-packs, discount shoes, and whole days in bed. Ray and I spent it talking and talking, speaking reams of absolute crap, but it filled up space, so I thought it must be important. Now that I don't have either of them, I keep sitting bolt upright in bed, on the tube, at the cinema, and thinking, "So what am I going to do next?" I think of something fabulous to do, but nine times out of ten I don't do it, in case it's the wrong thing and I waste part of my life. Manny keeps instigating ice-cream frenzies, but I have lost the taste for it.

I tentatively put the scratched Kindness of Strangers single on the turntable. It was still awful. But I didn't miss him anymore. What will be will be. We wouldn't have been soulmates. He probably didn't even like me, with my lists and intricate dissection of the lyrics to "Like a Prayer." "Oh, Drew." I felt his name rise in my throat, then I gobbled it down again. It went slowly, sticking in my windpipe, stifling my breath.

I decided to write some bad poetry and, for the first time in days, got out of bed. I couldn't bring myself to take my nightie off, so I decided to keep it on. It didn't really look like a nightie, I reasoned. What is a nightie anyway? Just a pretty dress you put on for bed. Madonna wears corsets over her clothes. Why can't I wear a nightie to the park? Stuck in a tube tunnel, I had my answer: because, when you wear a nightie out into the world, everyone stares at you as if you are mad. Such hypocrisy. If I had cut up my arms, or starved my body, or injected myself with heroin, they could better recognise my badge of mental instability. But I don't like needles or razors and I do like food. So here is my madness, take it or leave it: I like to wear nightclothes during the day. That's how much I hate myself.

I had nothing with me, not even my keys. If I had had the foresight to bring my wallet, I would have ducked into the first M&S and bought myself a complete, non-nocturnal wardrobe. I felt very uncomfortable. This was supposed to be a film, but it had become a pop video. "So, Viva, your 'thing' will be wearing nighties out in public. And we'll, like, film you in normal situations amongst ordinary people to show how disjointed you are from this society. And can someone from makeup please put some gaffer-tape round her tits? I want them lifted higher."

I felt better when I reached the park. It is an acknowledged fact: Everyone in parks is mad. Tramps with matted hair spit from benches. Old men hide behind bushes and hiss. Watch out especially for small children on tricycles painted with lambs—they are crazy. I climbed high up to the top branch of the tree, where nobody could stare at me and I could stare at everyone. The branches were thick and strong and the top branch was only eight feet off the ground. It would have been a great place to talk about Sartre.

I crept through Belsize Park, letting the rain soak me, mingling with calm tears—fantastic, I thought, my life is officially a movie—walking slowly, deliberately so every drop caught me full on for the cameras. How much practice would it take before I knew my best angles and most flattering key-lights by heart? "North London Jew," Ray liked to mock. "Don't be such a chest-beating North London Jew," he would have said, if he could see me in my film. His argument was that he so thoroughly worshipped and adored the Jews that he felt entitled to be rude about them. After all, he practically was one. He was short and depressed, wasn't he? He said "The Jews" as if it were the name of a hot new sitcom.

I put Ray out of my thoughts in the rain and locked the door. He banged against the patio windows of my mind as I concentrated my attention on the two abandoned parties who were probably feeling even worse than me: Marcus and Tommy.

I walked back to the station, my hair starting to frizz in the heat. I perused the magazines at the news-stall as I waited for my train. Skyline were on three covers. All of them showed a close-up of Dillon's face, with the rest of the band in soft focus. Part of me wanted to see him. But the other part knows that if you have an amazing night with a new aquaintance, you should not try to repeat it. If you do, it will eventually become a carbon copy of itself so faint that it can barely be read. That's how relationships end: new aquaintances become old photocopies.

I felt incredibly low for my first week back in London. Depression is like falling in love for the first time. You honestly can't imagine that one day you might not feel that way. It's inconceivable that you might fall out of love and it's inconceivable that you could ever be happy again. I'm not talking about "Oh God, I'm so depressed" depression, which, being a teenager, I battle with every minute of the day. Or even the excruciating Ecstasy comedown depression that Treena had every Tuesday after her Saturday night on the town with Marcus. I mean, this thing that chokes your heart and nestles in your hair and won't go, no matter how often you wash it, no difference what colour you dye it. That's why there are so many hair-dye products on the market. Black hair will fix it all, no, ginger, no, ash blond, no, deep, gothy purple will change your life. There are so many shades of hair colour out there. They bring in about ten new ones a year.

According to the rules of courtship, if you're a girl and you want to get your guy, you must never, ever phone him and you must never let him end the conversation. Treena just walked out on my phone call. I guess she got distracted by a picture in the paper, or a cloud in the shape of Ireland, or a word in her head. She left me here, on the other end of the phone, babbling until I realised I couldn't hear her breath, and then crying, "Hello, hello, are you still there?" She has made my voice sound very shrill. I was always "the little girl with the deep voice"—that's what they called me at school. I loved it. I felt like a starlet with a Harry Cohen sobriquet. "The Oomph Girl" (Ann Sheridan). "The Magnificent Animal" (Joan Collins). "The Little Girl with the Deep Voice" (Viva Cohen). But now Manny says, "Oy, Viva, your voice is so squeaky lately."

Recovering from love is like falling down steps. You're a girl with balance. You're a compact and graceful mover. You think you've got your footing. But somehow you trip over your trouser leg and tumble to the bottom. Each time you're more frightened of the steps and the more you try not to think about it, the more you obsess until descending the stairs becomes your life. Where you're going and where you've been becomes irrelevant.

I feel like a broken record, scratched on my favourite song. I fell in love so hard, it's left me with a scratch on my brain. I should have handled this vinyl by the edges, without getting greasy fingerprints on it, like Manny always yells at me. But the cover was so pretty, I just whipped out the record and whammed it on. I know it's my fault for being a klutz. But how do you fix a record? You don't. That's why they invented CDs.

When I got home I was inexplicably consumed by the urge to speak to Tommy Belucci, to know for sure if he was as miserable as I was. He was. I got his number from Directories, and quickly wished I had left it alone. I never wanted to be in a position where I would have to feel sorry for Tommy

Belucci. He was so distraught, he didn't even sound surprised to hear from me.

"Have you, uh, seen Ray lately?" he asked desperately.

"No, not really. Not since he and Treena got together."

"No. Neither have I. He hasn't returned my phone calls. I guess he's been really busy. First flush of true love and all." He began to sob. "He was my whole life."

I couldn't think of anything nice to say, so I said, "Tommy, without being rude, you're in your forties, aren't you?"

He snivelled. "Yes."

"So you must have been doing something before you met Ray?"

"Yes," he answered testily.

"So you could go back to your old friends, your old life."

"But he's left me with nothing," he shrieked, hysterical. And I was so embarrassed for him, I had to scrunch my eyes tight shut. "I gave him all that time, five years of my life, and he's left me with nothing. It's okay for you, you had sex with him."

I gasped. "No I didn't."

"You didn't?" he asked, sniffing away snot.

"Christ, no."

"But . . ."

"But what?"

"But, he was in love with you."

My heart leaped into my throat, out of my mouth, and across to the other side of the room, where it perched on the couch, pumping blood on the cushions. "Tommy, don't say that. He was not." I clutched my chest. "He told you that?"

"He didn't have to tell me."

I went down to the kitchen, wearing my bra and knickers. Manny was sipping coffee, reading the newspaper and listening to the radio. It was as I was rooting around the fridge that it happened for the third time in as many weeks. "The time's coming up five-fifty. It's a swelteringly hot day and here's Don Henley with those 'Boys of Summer.'"

My reactions aren't as sharp as they were before I wasted them on Drew. I sunk into a chair, cracked open a Coke, and starting singing along.

"I can't tell you my love for you will still be strong, after the boys of summer have gone."

Manny looked up from his paper. "That's wrong."

"No it's not. I was in key."

"Your singing's lovely, but you got the words wrong. It's 'I *can* tell you.'"

"What?"

"It's 'I *can* tell you my love for you will still be strong, after the boys of summer have gone.'"

"No it isn't."

He laughed as if I were a small child with jam around her mouth. "Yes it is. It's about the rich kids who descend on the Hamptons for the summer and impress their town beauty with their flash cars, and about the local boy who will always love her, no matter what."

I held the Coke to my temple. "Are you sure about this?"

"Yes, Viva. I should know, I spent my childhood summers in the Hamptons."

I excused myself and crept into bed. It was so hot that I had taken the duvet off and was just using the sheets. I kicked my legs up and made myself a tent, with blue light coming through where the sheets were thin. Then I let the tent collapse and curled into a ball. The whole point of "Boys of Summer" is that it's about how love, in its purest form, should last no more than a season. It's a hymn to living for the moment, to loving until you can love no more and then stopping. It's about knowing when to call it a day, when your series is about to be cancelled. The bikini dissolving in the water. Except it's not, because I had heard the words wrong.

There was nothing I could do. That song was gone, dead. What a stupid, stupid record. I had lived my life a certain way because of those lyrics. What else had I misheard? Lying there I decided, "If it's 'I can tell you' and not 'I can't tell you,' then I don't want to live in this world. And there is nothing, nothing left for me to do. Except find a new record to mishear."

The more time passes, the more I hope I'm going to bump into Tommy in the street, and he'll let on that, actually, EVERYONE was in love with me. He'll take me for a coffee, and say, "You know, Drew was always in love with you. He was just too afraid to tell you," or "All Dillon's girlfriends have been like faxes of you," or "Treena has photos of you plastered all over the flat." But we have no mutual friends. There are no extras in my movies. How stupid of me. The crowd of extras is a great place for the troubled star to hide. Elizabeth Taylor did it at the height of Liz 'n' Dick mania. In 1969, she appeared, unbilled, in *Anne of the Thousand Days*, just a violet-eyed, double-lashed face in the crowd. I hear it was the happiest she ever was.

And then I remembered one extra.

I didn't have time to dress as anyone, and besides, all my

best clothes were still dirty from Vegas. I pulled on my one pair of jeans, a grey vest, the Adidas sneakers Treena had handed down, and a hooded sweatshirt Ray had lent me. My hair had grown too shaggy for me to try to be Elizabeth, so I pulled it back in a ponytail and rooted through my bag for the underground fare. The train was sweltering and I tied the sweatshirt around my waist. I ran up the stairs at Piccadilly and was so happy to be overground that I could barely smell the urine and discarded McDonald's.

In Uptown Records, Marcus was just shutting up shop for the day. I pressed my face to the glass and watched him count the takings from the till. He was wearing indigo denim dungarees with one strap unbuckled. If it didn't say TOMMY HILFIGER in huge letters across the chest pocket, I would have taken it for a giant toddler's romper suit. His hair matched his clothes, with one side of it braided into antennae and the other in a three-inch Afro. I waved at him and he cocked his antennae to a right angle. When he saw it was me, he smiled. The gold on his teeth caught the last rays of the day's sun.

About the Author

Emma Forrest is a twenty-two-year-old Londoner living in New York. From the age of fifteen, she divided her time between school and rock journalism. *Namedropper* has been translated into six languages and Forrest is now completing her second novel.